A beat of unexpected silence thrummed between them. One that said the tension between them signaled far more than mere friendship.

Finally, he nodded. "I suppose I could use a friend."

She ignored a sharp jab of misgiving. "Then it's a deal."

"Daddy." David snagged his father's attention. "Can we make a vegetable garden?"

"I like pink flowers," Annie told her.

"Not me," David objected.

"I don't know, son. There are few things in this world as incredible as a perfect rose or a beautiful woman, and, usually, you'll find the two together."

Something warm curled in Katherine's stomach. She knew Michael Carlson was a special man, but she hadn't expected a soul filled with romance. As she looked at the Carlsons, she envied the special relationship they shared. One she'd always wanted to be part of. And once again Katherine was standing on the outside looking in.

Books by Bonnie K. Winn

Love Inspired

A Family All Her Own #158

BONNIE K. WINN

A hopeless romantic, Bonnie K. Winn naturally turned to romance writing. This seasoned author of historical and contemporary romance has won numerous awards, including having been voted one of the Top Ten Romance Authors in America, according to *Affaire de Coeur.* Living in the foothills of the Rockies gives Bonnie plenty of inspiration and a touch of whimsy, as well. She shares her life with her husband, son and a spunky Westie terrier. Bonnie welcomes mail from her readers. You can write to her c/o Steeple Hill Books, 300 E. 42nd St., 6th Floor, New York, NY 10017.

A Family All Her Own
Bonnie K. Winn

Published by Steeple Hill Books™

STEEPLE HILL BOOKS

Steeple
Hill™

ISBN 0-373-87165-1

A FAMILY ALL HER OWN

Printed in U.S.A.

Hope deferred makes the heart sick,
but desire fulfilled is a tree of life.

—*Proverbs* 13:12

Dedicated to my mother, Tex Yedlovsky, who taught me the value of faith, and who showed me every day in every way a lifetime of her belief.

ACKNOWLEDGMENTS

To Ann Leslie Tuttle and Tracy Farrell for sharing that faith. And to Karen Winkel, pastor of the Bountiful Community Church, for sharing the truth about being a woman in the ministry. Any flights of fiction are strictly my own.

Prologue

"So. What do you do for a living?"

Although the conversation had been going well up until that moment, Katherine Blake glanced at the attractive man with the inviting grin and felt her hopes evaporate. She had visited Nichols Grocery many times, but this was the first time she'd met such a good-looking, apparently eligible man at the store.

Unfortunately she had heard this particular question before. And it was always a killer.

Guessing how he would react, still Katherine smiled. "Actually I'm the minister of Rosewood Community Church."

The man's face shifted from confusion to incredulity to discomfort in under fifteen seconds. It was a new record. At the same time, he stepped backward at her off-putting admission.

"Right. Maybe I'll see you there sometime."

"I look forward to it," she replied, knowing the flirtatious encounter had skidded to a halt and it was time to change hats. "All are welcome."

Nodding, the man edged away. Clearly he wanted to escape. Katherine's lips curled in an ironic smile. Apparently the man thought she might come after him. *Not to worry,* Katherine wanted to tell him. She recognized that uncomfortable look, one often tinged with pity. The men she had met over the years couldn't understand why a woman without a hump or a third eye would choose to become a minister. As a result they treated her much like a nun out of her habit—sort of a non-woman, one they couldn't get away from fast enough.

Katherine couldn't squash a familiar feeling of hurt. She was accustomed to the reaction, but she also longed for that one special man who would respond differently, who would embrace the choice she had made. One who wouldn't be too intimidated to embrace her, as well.

It wouldn't be this man, though. Mr. Good-looking and Eligible was wheeling his cart away as though piloting a race car in the Indy 500.

Unfortunately, he wasn't that good a driver.

In his haste to escape, the man crashed into the week's special: canned tomatoes. Cans toppled and slid down with a force only towering stacks of tin could achieve.

Unable to stop the avalanche, Katherine gasped as the momentum continued, dismantling the top half of the display. Dozens of cans crashed into her cart while others rolled haphazardly down the aisle.

Then, as she watched in stunned disbelief, the man sped away from the scene of his crime.

Tempted to throw a can after the retreating coward, instead Katherine swallowed an equally unflattering thought and bent to pick up the mess.

Suddenly, someone knelt down beside her. For a moment she thought her coward had repented. But glancing up, she met a far more handsome face, concern written in his deep blue eyes.

"Are you all right?" he asked.

At the same time, three small children surrounded them, gaping at her in wide-eyed astonishment.

The lone boy was the only one to speak as he stared at the mess. "Wow!"

"Are you okay?" the man repeated.

Dragging her gaze from the children, Katherine met the man's eyes. "Yes, I'm fine. The cart got the worst of it."

"This is really cool," the boy told her in admiration. Then, before either his father or Katherine could anticipate his next move, he pushed the man's cart forward, toppling the remainder of the display, most of which fell into Katherine's cart.

Her lips twitched when the child crowed with glee at the mini-disaster. It was a remarkable sight—especially to the young driver.

"David!" his father admonished.

The boy shrugged and said with childlike reasoning, "The thing was already coming down, Daddy."

It looked as though the man were silently counting to ten. "And now you've doubled the damage. Tell the lady you're sorry."

"Sorry," the youngster told her, not looking particularly repentant. Instead, he looked even more impressed by the massive spillage.

Katherine clamped down on her bottom lip and tried to look appropriately serious. "No damage done. I got into my share of accidents when I had my beginner's permit, too."

"He's not old enough to drive," one of the girls told her in a conspiratorial tone.

"And David knows better," the father added, his glance rebuking the boy.

Katherine met the man's eyes, again noticing their deep blue color. "As I said, no harm, no foul." She turned her attention back to the cans. "If we all pitch in, it won't take long to put this back together."

A harried stock boy approached. "It's okay, lady. I can do that."

"We insist on helping," the man replied. Then he directed his compelling gaze to Katherine, again impressing her with both his looks and his consideration.

Now, why couldn't he be single? Katherine lamented. Instead of the ill-mannered boor who had left her with the disaster. But that was her luck, always had been. The good ones were either taken or uninterested. Like this one. He had a small flock of children, and a discreet glance at his left hand showed a simple gold band. *Lucky woman,* Katherine thought with a silent sigh of longing.

Soon, with all the large and small hands helping, the cans were restacked. And the stock boy insisted on completing the display.

Grateful, Katherine smiled at them all. Then, impulsively, she held out her hand to young David. "I'm Katherine Blake. It was nice to run into you."

The boy grinned at her choice of words. "I'm David Carlson." He shook her hand, obviously pleased to be treated like a grown-up.

His father hesitated a moment, then offered his hand, too. "Michael Carlson."

Katherine accepted his handshake, startled by an unexpected shiver of awareness at the contact. Trying not to be obvious, she pulled back, alarmed at her reaction to a married man. She was accustomed to shaking many hands each week. It went with the professional territory. Why had this one seemed so different?

One of the little girls tugged on her father's sleeve.

"This is Annie." The man shifted his hands, placing one on the other girl's shoulder. "And Tessa."

The girls squirmed, grinned, and then dug the toes of matching purple tennis shoes against the grocery cart.

"You two look like you're the same age," Katherine replied, thinking one of the girls looked familiar, but she couldn't place where she'd seen Tessa before. "Fraternal twins?"

The girls giggled in obvious delight.

"Actually they're friends, not sisters," the man explained. "But they might as well be twins. They're always together."

Katherine winked at the girls in understanding. "It's a girl thing, isn't it."

They nodded, grinned again, and then bounced up and down.

Seeing that they were still blocking the aisle and that the stock boy was looking even more harried, Katherine pulled her cart backward out of the melee. "Well, it was great meeting all of you."

The man nodded, but the children waved enthusiastically as she headed the opposite way down the aisle. Now, those were the kinds of conquest she could handle, Katherine decided wryly—the under ten-year-old variety. Kids and safe, married men.

Chapter One

The smallish town of Rosewood blossomed in the summer. Located outside Houston, the village-turned-town was situated on the gradually sloping lands that marked the approach of the Texas hill country. Children, playing with abandon, filled the streets and parks, euphoric with the months of freedom stretching out before them.

Katherine Blake felt equally enthusiastic about summer. Especially since it meant vacation Bible School this first week of June. It was one of her favorite activities at the church. There was much to love about being minister of the warm, caring congregation, but there was something so very special about anything involving the children.

And she really loved it when she got to sub in one of their classes. She rarely had the opportunity to step out of her administrative role. However, because they were short of volunteers, everyone had been reined in to help on this first day. And Katherine had drawn the class of five-year-olds.

Surely it was one of the Lord's many wonders—the amount of energy a room full of five-year-olds could generate. With no children of her own, Katherine appreciated every moment of her time with the many who belonged to the church. And she tried not to think about how much she longed for children of her own.

"Katherine, can you round up the paints and brushes for the art project? Oh, and the clay, too. I want to get started and take attendance."

"I'll get right on it, Donna." Katherine didn't mind the grunt work. She admired Donna Hobbs, the teacher of the class. Twenty-seven years old, bubbly, a pretty blonde, she was one of the best Sunday School teachers in the church.

As Katherine collected art supplies, she checked out the children still entering the classroom. As they continued parading inside, she suddenly recognized two of the miniature faces. Tessa and Annie from the grocery store collision!

It dawned on Katherine why Tessa had looked so familiar. She was new to the church—her family had just joined recently. The Spencers had changed churches because they wanted a stronger youth program for their family, which included a teenager and two younger children. Tessa had been visiting her grandparents when the family joined Rosewood. Katherine had only glimpsed the youngest child last Sunday, when her parents had retrieved her from the children's church service.

Pleased to see her new friends, Katherine approached them. "Tessa, Annie. Great to see you."

"Hi!" they greeted her in unison, still somewhat shy. But their grins were welcoming.

"Are you the teacher?" Tessa asked, her face puckered in anticipation.

"Actually, I'm the helper."

"Daddy says I'm his best helper," Annie confided, losing a touch of her shyness.

Katherine smiled as she met Annie's large blue eyes, which were filled with bashful pride. The child was a charmer. "I'm sure you are the very best helper," Katherine agreed.

"I help, too!" Tessa added, not wanting to be outdone by her friend.

"Oh, I'm sure you do," Katherine replied seriously, although her eyes danced with amusement. What a pair!

Since Donna was trying to quiet the class, Katherine left them with a wink. But throughout the morning, she found her gaze wandering toward the winsome duo.

The time spent with the five-year-olds was as much fun as Katherine had anticipated. When Donna called for the closing prayer, Katherine was nearly as disappointed as the children to see the class end.

A few parents were lined up in the hall, chatting among themselves as the session ended. Donna had asked Katherine to man the classroom door while she escorted some of the children out to waiting cars at the front drive.

Glancing down the hallway, Katherine recognized Annie's father striding down the hallway. His purposeful gait didn't match his surroundings. Michael Carlson looked like he belonged atop a steed or perhaps the modern-day version—a massive Harley. She shook her head at the notion.

"Mr. Carlson—" she began with a smile.

But he cut her off. "I'm here to pick up Annie and Tessa."

Although his words were controlled, she could see that he was angry. She wondered why.

"Of course. They're right here. We certainly enjoyed having them today."

"This one time had better last Annie."

Confused, she watched as he began to shepherd the girls out of the room. She snagged his sleeve. "Mr. Carlson? I don't understand. Is something wrong?"

"Annie was here without permission. Tessa's mother didn't mean anything by it, but Annie won't be back."

"But why not? She seemed to enjoy it so much and—"

"We don't go to church. Ever."

Katherine felt his distress in her own soul. "Oh, surely you can't mean that!"

"I said it and I meant it."

"Perhaps if you and your wife discussed it—"

"My wife's dead."

Stunned, Katherine was silenced for a moment, even though her eyes flicked to the ring he still wore. "I'm sorry. I didn't mean to be insensitive. But I do hope you'll reconsider about Annie." She paused, sensing his loss, knowing words couldn't dilute it. "I'll be praying for you and your family."

His blue eyes met hers, the darkness in them hiding what she guessed was a wealth of pain. "Don't bother."

The children in tow, Michael strode through the hallways, slowing down only long enough to accommodate Annie's and Tessa's shorter legs.

He kept up the pace as they left the church and drove rapidly toward home.

But he couldn't stop thinking about Katherine Blake. He had been aware of her in the grocery store when they met. In fact, she'd lingered in his mind. And again today when he spotted her, he'd felt an unwelcome jab of attraction. It wasn't something he was ready for.

Michael could still see the compassion in Katherine's eyes. But he had seen similar expressions all too often after Ruth had died. He didn't need the pity of do-gooders, certainly not from lady Sunday School teachers.

He and Ruth had just moved to Rosewood and only attended the local Methodist Church a few times when she became ill. Staying home to care for her and the kids, Michael hadn't realized then it would be one of the last times he'd enter a church.

No, he and his kids didn't need anything from anyone…not anymore. There had been a time when he had begged, pleaded. But that time was gone, never to be recovered.

Once at home, Michael took over for the baby-sitter, Mrs. Goode, who was happy for the rare opportunity to leave early. Tessa and Annie retreated to the world of Barbie dolls and make-believe. His son, however, was more practical.

"Dad, I'm hungry," David announced, shifting from one leg to the other in an impatient dance.

"I know. You'll have to wait until it's cooked."

David tried to finagle. "We could order pizza."

"By the time the pizza could get here, I'll have dinner cooked."

"But if we order pizza, you wouldn't *have* to cook. You could read the newspaper or watch TV."

"Nice try, David. But you need your vegetables."

David sighed, a heartfelt groan of disappointment. "Then, can I eat at Billy's?"

Michael stared suspiciously at his son. "Any special reason?"

"Well..." David hedged.

"Why?" Michael insisted.

"His mom's a *really* good cook," David finally admitted.

And it went without saying that Michael wasn't. So much about their lives had changed since Ruth's death. So many things he felt his children had been cheated out of—things he couldn't compensate for or replace. But he had to try.

"It's important that we eat together as a family. Why don't you see if Billy wants to come over, instead?"

"Uh, if he does, could we have something *good?* Like pizza?"

"We already covered that, David. No pizza. So, you going to call Billy?"

"Nah." With seven-year-old resilience, David scampered away.

Dinner was a quiet affair. The children picked at the overdone pork chops and soggy cabbage. Clearly David could picture the pizza he'd been denied. And Michael dreaded the difficult task ahead of him.

Once the dishes were stacked in the dishwasher, Michael approached Annie, who was in her room enthralled with her new toy stove. "Hey, princess, you have a minute?"

She looked up, her sweet smile melting his heart. "Sure, Daddy. You want to play?"

Obligingly, Michael sat down next to his daughter, trying to fit his long legs into the cramped floor space between the stove and all its accessories: miniature bowls, pans, silverware and mixer. "What are we playing?"

"Dessert. I'm baking a *huge* cake."

Feeling his love for his precious daughter swelling, Michael smiled. "What kind of cake?"

"Chocolate!" she chirped, opening the door to the play oven, her imagination filling in where reality stopped.

"Good. My favorite."

Again she looked up at him. "I know. That's why it's chocolate."

His heart completely undone, Michael accepted the small plastic plate filled with part of an Oreo cookie. He took a bite, then waited a moment. "This is delicious, Annie."

Obviously pleased, she broke into a grin. "Thanks, Daddy."

For a few moments he enjoyed the bites of cookie, accompanied by water served in tiny teacups. But he knew he had to tell Annie, to get this over, even though he dreaded doing so. "Princess, I need to talk to you."

"About what, Daddy?"

He paused. "Honey, you can't go with Tessa to vacation Bible School tomorrow."

At first Annie's small face reflected only confusion. "But why not, Daddy?"

"We don't go to church," he replied, not wanting to meet the questions in her eyes.

Then her lips quivered as her face crumpled. "Why can't I, Daddy? Tessa gets to go. And she's my very best friend in the whole world!"

"I know. But Tessa's family belongs to the church. We don't."

"Tessa's mom said that's okay. That Jesus wants everyone to come to His house."

Michael's throat worked, remembering a time he, too, had believed that to be true. "Annie, it's different for us. So, I'm sorry, but you can't go."

Tears rolled down Annie's cheeks. "But I want to go, Daddy!"

Again Michael fought a wave of emotion, swamped by the bitter irony of his words. "Honey, we don't always get what we want in this life."

But Annie was beyond logic. Crying loudly now, her eyes and words accused him. "But you could let me go if you wanted to!"

Feeling helpless, Michael hated to hurt his child, but he could not budge on this point. When it had mattered most, God had let him down, let them all down. And Michael couldn't ever forget it.

The following morning Katherine watched the children pouring through the hallways, searching for little Annie Carlson. She had prayed for the troubled family, hoping the Lord would soften Michael's heart.

Brightening, she spotted Tessa Spencer. Still searching, she didn't see her other young friend. But maybe they hadn't come together.

When Tessa was close enough, Katherine knelt down beside her. "Morning, Tessa. How are you?"

"Okay," Tessa replied without her usual exuberance.

"Where's Annie today?"

"She couldn't come. Her daddy wouldn't let her."

Katherine suspected her own disappointment equaled Tessa's. "Maybe he'll change his mind before vacation Bible School ends. We have almost two weeks left."

Tessa didn't look convinced. "Her daddy said she couldn't come back, ever."

Katherine winced. The man was a tough case. Then, seeing how forlorn little Tessa was without her friend, Katherine reached for her hand, linking it with her own. "How about if you're my special helper today?"

"But I thought *you* were the helper. What would I do?"

"Help me pass out the art supplies, get the juice and cookies ready."

Looking somewhat comforted, Tessa nodded. "Okay." Yet she kept her hand within the safe confines of Katherine's.

Michael Carlson's stubbornness was hurting two little girls very much. Katherine could only imagine how much he was hurting himself.

It had been a long day, one which Michael had spent thinking mostly of his daughter and how he'd denied her request. He couldn't erase the image of her tears. But he also knew his children were adaptable.

Regrettably, it was late. Michael had hoped to be home earlier, but the workday hadn't cooperated. He hated that his contracting business often meant working long hours. It was a double-edged sword. As a single parent he had sole financial and emotional responsibility for his children. Yet it seemed he was always sacrificing one for the other.

And Mrs. Goode, the baby-sitter, was getting tired of working overtime. She had warned him again this evening when he'd come home that if it continued, he'd be looking for another caregiver.

The house was far too quiet. He expected it from Annie—he knew she was still upset. Mrs. Goode had confirmed that. But David could be counted on for his share of noise no matter what else was going on in the house.

The sitter had reported that the kids were in their rooms. Michael hoped David wasn't brewing up another excruciating scheme. His son was long on imagination and fearlessness, but short on caution.

Michael poked his head into David's room. His son was organizing rows of toy soldiers. "Formulating a battle plan?"

David shrugged.

Concerned, Michael stepped inside, then crouched down beside David. "Is something wrong, son?"

David continued to line up the green plastic warriors. "Annie's still crying."

"Still?"

"Yeah. She's been crying a lot."

Michael frowned. "Mrs. Goode said she'd been quiet today."

"Yeah, well she didn't want Mrs. Goode to see her cry."

Placing an arm around David's shoulders, Michael hugged him. "Thanks for telling me. Caring about your family is a true sign of responsibility."

David shrugged. "I don't like seeing Annie cry."

"Me, either. A man never wants to see a girl in

tears." *Or to be the cause of them,* Michael reminded himself.

"I wish things were like they used to be," David mumbled. "When Mommy was here."

When he was certain David was all right, Michael hurried down the hall. Pausing at the doorway of Annie's room, he was sickened by the sound of her quiet sobs. In a few quick strides he was inside, scooping his daughter off the bed and into his arms.

She resisted for a moment, and then her baby-soft arms wound around his neck. "Oh, Daddy!"

Her words and agony crept into his heart. "Shush, Annie, it'll be okay."

He cradled her until the sobs lessened into a few hiccups. "Annie, you mustn't go on like this."

"But Daddy, I want to be with Tessa and Katherine. I want to visit Jesus's house."

The pain ripped through him at her innocent words. "Oh, Annie…"

"I don't want to be left out again!"

"Left out?"

"I don't have a mommy to help in kindergarten or Sunshine Girls. And I'm the only one. I don't want to always be the only one!"

Heart fracturing, Michael held her close. He knew Annie and David desperately missed their mother, but it hadn't occurred to him that the lack of one would make the children feel singled out. And now, denying his daughter vacation Bible School was making her feel even more an outsider.

Though he was a strong man of principle, Michael didn't want those principles to inflict further pain on his children. And Annie had cried for nearly twenty-

four hours. She wasn't simply throwing a tantrum—
she was deeply hurt.

He pulled a handkerchief from his pocket and ten-
derly wiped the tears from Annie's face. "I think I
could use some hot cocoa. How about you?"

She nodded, her lips still wobbling. "What about
Bible School?"

He lifted Annie into his arms and carried her from
the room. "I guess we'd better talk about that some
more." He smoothed back the hair from her flushed
face. "Maybe we can work out something."

After all, vacation Bible School only lasted two
weeks. If it meant that much to Annie, he could bear
it for a short time. It wasn't as though he planned on
signing up hook, line and sinker. In two weeks they
would walk away from the church, just as the Lord
had walked away from them.

The next morning Katherine reprised her role as
teacher's helper for the five-year-old class. Even
though Donna had enlisted another volunteer, Katherine managed to head the other woman in the direction of a different class. She simply had to learn what
was going to happen with Tessa and Annie.

Praying about it the previous evening, Katherine
had asked for guidance. Was it time for her to pay
Michael Carlson a visit in her official capacity? Or
should she wait and see if he relented on his own?

Anxiously studying the doorway of the classroom,
Katherine spotted Tessa. A happy-looking Tessa. Not
a foot behind her, Annie appeared. Her shy, sweet
expression was in place, along with a blossoming
smile.

Sweeping forward, Katherine enveloped both girls in her own smile. "So. The twins are back in action!"

Matching grins replied.

"That's right. You're not *really* twins," Katherine continued.

The girls giggled.

"We're not really even sisters," Tessa reminded her in a loud whisper.

"Sometimes friends are like sisters, though, aren't they? Almost better, because we get to choose them."

Annie's sweet smile grew. "I would always pick Tessa."

"And I would pick Annie," Tessa added loyally, not to be outdone.

"Then, I'd say you're both very lucky. Come on in. I think we're about ready to get started."

The girls blended in, and the lively session went well. The time flew quickly, and soon it was time for the parents to pick up the children.

Katherine watched for Michael Carlson with a mix of anticipation and dread. She wondered how he would act today. She hoped he realized that he was serving Annie's best interests in allowing her to attend vacation Bible School.

Since Katherine had lived in Rosewood less than a year, she hadn't met everyone in town. And she was certain she would have remembered him. It was easy to spot him in the crowd. His tall, well-muscled build set him apart. He was a handsome, distinctive-looking man in every sense. Thick, dark hair at odds with his blue, blue eyes...and features that were arresting, strong, memorable. No wonder she had been so aware of him at their first meeting.

It took a giant dose of conscience to remember that

his need was spiritual, not romantic. Not that she had forgotten. But she couldn't shake that initial spark of attraction.

Compromising, she simply smiled. "It's good to see you, Mr. Carlson. We were very happy to have Annie with us today."

Obviously ill at ease, he avoided her gaze. "I haven't changed how I feel, but she had her heart set on coming here."

"I think you'll both be glad she did."

He didn't reply, but Katherine suspected what he wanted to say—that her attendance was against his better judgment.

Instead he absently ran his fingers over the old-fashioned light switch just inside the door.

"I guess they haven't made that kind of switch in years," she commented rather lamely, wishing she could find just the right words to reach this man.

"You're right." His fingers paused over a ragged patch in the wire that ran up the wall. "Is this the original system?"

She shrugged, her knowledge of building structure nonexistent. "Probably."

"You should get someone to check it out." Again his fingers lingered over a frayed wire. "It might not be safe."

"I'll mention it to the Deacons' committee."

"Good."

At that moment, Annie and Tessa rushed up to the doorway, all smiles.

Katherine told them to fetch their backpacks, then caught Michael's gaze again. "Whatever your reasons, you made them both very happy." She swallowed. "Actually, all three of us. And for that, I thank you."

Meeting his gaze, she saw something unexpected there—a light she couldn't quite define, but something that seemed to reach out between the two of them.

The girls returned, bouncing and bubbling with energy. Knowing it was uncertain ground, Katherine didn't press about seeing Annie again the following day, She had glimpsed the love Michael held for his daughter. Katherine doubted he could deny permission for her to return.

Somewhere in the exchange, she had glimpsed something of Michael Carlson, as well.

Just then he paused, turning back. "It's you I should thank."

Before she could reply, one of the other parents reached the classroom. "Afternoon, Pastor."

Acknowledging the greeting, Katherine glimpsed the shock in Michael's expression and could imagine the mental wheels whirling.

Katherine wanted to reach out and detain him, to prevent him from walking away. Impulsively, she blurted out the first thing she could think of. "There's a picnic!"

Michael's eyes widened but he didn't speak.

"On Sunday afternoon," Katherine continued. "It's open to everyone."

Michael's lips tightened.

Still Katherine rushed on. "It's not a service, just lunch on the lawn. The kids really enjoy it, and even the adults—"

"Thank you for the invitation, Pastor," Michael replied frostily.

It didn't take a mind reader to see he was angered by the invitation, especially since it had been delivered in front of his daughter. Katherine mentally pedaled faster, trying to think of a way to smooth over the words. "Actually, we're having a picnic here in vacation Bible School tomorrow, in case you can't make the one on Sunday."

Annie and Tessa both looked excited at the prospect.

"If you'll have the girls each pack a sack lunch, we'll provide drinks and dessert," Katherine continued. "There's a note with Annie's Bible story."

Tessa bounced a bit on her brightly colored tennis shoes. "Wow. Two picnics!"

Meeting Michael's stern expression, Katherine felt her diplomacy falter. And guessed she'd just hit rock bottom on his list.

Chapter Two

What was it about that church woman that got under his skin? Michael wondered when he got home. It wasn't just that she had a colossal talent for saying absolutely the worst thing.

He'd noticed, again, that she wore no rings on her left hand. That wasn't all he'd noticed. Her intelligent brown eyes had softened, seeming to see beyond the surface. It was disturbing, yet at the same time intriguing.

Michael wondered what her story was. How in the world had such an attractive woman come to be a minister? He ignored a niggling voice that said he once would have admired her choice, the strength of character it required.

But he didn't linger over that last thought. Grudgingly he admitted that she radiated energy. He just wished she wouldn't direct it all at trying to get his family to attend vacation Bible School and church picnics.

"Daddy!" David charged into the kitchen at full steam.

Pleased, Michael stooped down to pick up his son.

After a quick hug, David wriggled to get back down. He was growing so fast, Michael realized. Not too many hugging years left.

"Daddy," David repeated. "I want to go tomorrow, too!"

"Too?" Michael asked, his mind on what to prepare for dinner. Maybe he would relent and order pizza this once.

"With Annie!"

Michael stopped thinking about pepperoni versus combo, and concentrated on what his son was saying. With Annie? To vacation Bible School? At the *church?*

Feeling sucker-punched, Michael took a fortifying breath. "What do you mean, David?"

"Annie just told me about her day. It sounds fun, Daddy!"

"What kind of reason is that?" Realizing how idiotic he'd just sounded, Michael placed one hand on David's shoulder. "You don't want to horn in on your little sister and her friend."

Puzzled, David stared at him. "Huh?"

Michael's eyes flickered shut for a moment. What was he doing? He'd always encouraged his children to interact together. In fact, he'd taught David to include his younger sister whenever possible.

So he took another tack. "This isn't for you, David."

"Then, why can Annie go?"

Why, indeed? Because his daughter's tears had gotten to him. Because he hadn't believed things would

get so out of control. Because he thought he could
stop his children's curiosity and order their thoughts.

"David." He tried again. "I don't think this vacation Bible School thing is for you."

"But why not?" David screwed his face into a
heartfelt grimace.

*Because I don't want you to be hurt when every-
thing you learn to count on betrays you.*

"Daddy?" David implored.

"Why don't we think about it some more?" Michael suggested, knowing it was a losing proposition,
knowing he could do little to change that.

"But I wanna go tomorrow!" David protested.

Michael knew he couldn't rationalize, even to himself, that he would allow his daughter to attend but
not his son. It wouldn't be fair, and David knew it as
well as Michael did.

Defeat was tromping over him with relentless abandon.

"Please, Daddy? Please?"

"I was thinking about ordering pizza," Michael
said weakly.

But David wouldn't be distracted. "I had some at
Billy's. Can I go tomorrow?"

Michael had lost and he knew it. "Why don't we
see how you feel tomorrow?"

"I'll still wanna go," David insisted.

And Michael didn't doubt for a moment that his
son would. Again he thought of Katherine Blake. It
seemed since he'd met her, she'd started an impossible landslide. And now he had to figure out how to
halt it.

The following afternoon Katherine could see the
trepidation in Michael's face. Not only had his daugh-

ter attended vacation Bible School, but so had his impish son. And clearly, David had enjoyed the session.

Just as clearly, both of his children were loving the Thursday afternoon picnic. Unfortunately, the same couldn't be said of their father. Michael looked like a man caught in the crosshairs of his own making.

While other parents either relaxed at the tables or lounged on the grass with their offspring, Michael sat with rigid precision, as though expecting disaster. For a fleeting moment Katherine wished she hadn't issued the invitation. But she knew she had had to take this step.

She also had to take another.

"Mr. Carlson?"

He met her eyes and she admired that it was an unflinching gaze.

"Yes?"

"It's just a picnic." She gestured toward the swing set and slide where some of the children, including Annie and David, were playing. "And it's good for them to have other kids to play with." When he didn't reply, she pushed a bit more. "Don't you think so?"

"Pastor, I'm sure you mean well—"

"Katherine," she interrupted gently. All her parishioners were on a first-name basis with her. "Call me Katherine."

For a moment that nameless, undefined tension hung in the silence.

Then he spoke, but for Katherine the timbre of his voice only increased the tension. "Katherine."

Why did he have to say it that way, with an inflection that seemed to ring in the quiet?

Swallowing, she managed to secure the smile that had faded from her lips. "That's better."

"Not necessarily." His tone wasn't antagonistic, but the resignation tinged with bitterness seemed even worse. "I don't want to get to know you, *Katherine,* to get on a first-name basis. It's not personal. It's necessary."

Even though he maintained it wasn't personal, inwardly Katherine flinched. Why did she always champion the impossible causes? And why was she attracted to the impossible men? Ones who could never be part of her future.

Katherine glanced again toward the playground area. "You're doing a remarkable job with your children."

His expression grew wry. "You think so?"

Concerned, she drew her gaze from the children and back to Michael. "You don't?"

"They're missing a lot. Things I can't do and can't make up for. Things only their mother can provide."

"But you're providing love. That's what they need the most."

"I'll be sure to tell Annie that when she's in tears because she's the only one in Sunshine Girls without a mother for mother-daughter day."

Katherine swallowed her immediate response. It would be too pat, a cop-out she wasn't willing to take. Instead she glanced again at his children. "They're so beautiful, and seem so perfect. But it's what you don't see that hurts."

Michael looked at her in surprise. "No platitudes?"

"Would you want one?"

For a moment his mouth edged upward a fraction. "I've had more than my share."

"I imagine you have." She drew an unsmiling face in the droplets of condensation that clung to her paper cup. "I'm sorry about the picnic. My intentions were good, but I didn't mean to put you on the spot."

"I've been on the spot since their mother died."

Katherine added eyebrows to the face on the cup. "Has that been very long ago?"

"A year-and-a-half," he admitted bitterly.

It was as though his voicing the fact made it that much more painful.

"You miss her very much," Katherine said gently.

He acknowledged this silently.

"How did you meet her?" Katherine asked.

He looked surprised at the question. "At a church mixer, actually. We lived in the same small town, but her family had just moved there."

"You were young then?"

"In retrospect, very. At the time I didn't think so. I was all of twenty-one. But I knew the first time I met Ruth, she was the one for me." His eyes took on a faraway expression. "She was so sweet, never had an unkind thought for anyone. And it was genuine, nothing she put on to impress people." He laughed briefly, a little caustic sound. "When she got sick, she didn't complain. Her concern was for us, especially David and Annie. She was worried about how *we* would cope."

"Are the children adjusting?"

"I'm not sure that ever happens."

Katherine guessed it would, but it wasn't her place to say so. Since Michael was pushing the church away, she knew that any pushing of her own would only make him that much more resistant. "Annie's a sweet child."

"She's a lot like her mother," Michael acknowledged. "Ruth was all about giving and caring."

"That's a special legacy."

"Pity that's all Annie has. A legacy, instead of a flesh-and-blood mother."

Katherine winced before she could stop herself.

"Too graphic an image for you?"

Katherine considered her next words, then plunged on nevertheless. "No. But I was wondering if it's an image you portray for David and Annie at home."

"This a typical preacher's question?"

"No," she replied truthfully. "Not in any sense."

"Since you're being candid, I will be, too. No, I don't insist on daily morbid reminders for my kids. They remember their mother, they know what they've lost. I want to help them, to make it easier, not more painful."

"Which is what you've done by bringing them here," Katherine said.

"You're very certain of yourself, aren't you?"

She nodded. "It's a curse, I'm afraid. Most mothers in my neighborhood encouraged their daughters to be meek, gentle and unassuming. My mother taught me to be courageous, outspoken and very much myself." She shrugged with a touch of undisguised irony. "I didn't break a mold. My mother refused to allow me to even glimpse the mold. In fact, she was convinced it had been broken and discarded years before."

"So your mother was very influential?"

Katherine smiled, keeping the rueful, not as optimistic, thoughts to herself. "She certainly was."

"Then, tell me, Katherine. How is it you think my children should be able to grow up without a mother of their own?"

Katherine pondered Michael's words long after the picnic ended, long after she'd bid his family a goodnight. Even now, Katherine wondered if she should have told him the complete truth about her mother and the uneven upbringing she'd had.

As a pioneering female minister, Victoria Blake had possessed definite opinions and convictions about many things. One of those had been to teach Katherine the value of giving to others, the importance of generosity and service.

But there had been a downside, one Katherine didn't like to dwell on. Her mother's strong personality and equally dominant occupation had been difficult to balance with marriage. Everything in the family had paled in comparison to her duties and obligations. Family vacations were postponed, often never taken. Time alone with either Katherine or her father, Edward, was nonexistent.

Edward's career was always downplayed, given second consideration after Victoria's. And after a time it was apparent that Victoria's only true concern was her ministry.

Katherine's father tried for as long as he could, but after a time he could not continue to take a backseat to his wife's ministry. Their marriage didn't so much break up as break *down* from lack of care, communication, and time spent with each other.

While Katherine despaired over the loss of family, her mother was philosophical. Victoria wasn't bitter toward Edward, instead believing that her sacrifice was worth the rewards of her career. In Victoria's opinion, the help and guidance she gave her congregation ranked higher in importance than her marriage. It never occurred to her that the Lord would have expected her to value her own family, as well.

Despite her mother's flaws, Katherine had never doubted Victoria's dedication to the Lord. Nor had those flaws affected Katherine's faith. Both of her parents had given her a long-lasting legacy of deep-rooted belief that even their individual mistakes couldn't weaken.

Yet she had often wondered what would have happened if her mother had simply given in a little bit, allowed her husband a place in her life. But that hadn't happened. It wasn't in Victoria Blake to give in, to consider that she might be wrong.

Consequently, Katherine wondered at her own ability to have a successful relationship. She had seen firsthand what happened to a marriage when one of the partners was a headstrong female minister.

Just like she was.

And now she was trying to counsel a man whose children no longer had a mother. How could she possibly give him unbiased advice? How could she explain that not every maternal legacy was a good one?

But then, she didn't think Michael Carlson wanted to hear anything from her. Which was going to make it that much more difficult to tell him that the following evening was a special gathering for all the parents and children to recap the first week of vacation Bible School. It was something they had discussed during class, something that all the children were excited about. Something she didn't want Annie and David to miss out on.

Grappling with the dilemma, Katherine could think of only one possible course of action.

However, even after she got into her car and pointed it in the direction of the Carlson home, Katherine wondered if she was doing the right thing. And as she turned into the driveway, the doubts were barreling through her mind.

And when she reached for the doorbell, an entire colony of butterflies chose to migrate to her stomach.

That wasn't in her nature. She'd never been a timid soul. If anything, she was too assertive. Besides, this was a pastoral call, one to benefit the children.

Then Michael pulled open the door and all her thoughts turned to mush.

"Hello," he greeted her, the solitary word as much a question as a statement.

Luckily, a fraction of her composure returned. "Good evening. I hope I'm not interrupting your dinner."

He hesitated, then opened the door a bit wider. "No. Actually, we just finished, and I was doing the dishes."

"Let me help!" she offered hastily, latching on to that excuse.

"Pardon me?"

She smiled through her nerves. "Really, let me help. Since I live alone I don't have much KP duty."

"So you're going door-to-door to find some?"

"You must admit, I could corner the market. Not too much competition," Katherine countered, knowing she must sound every bit as foolish as she felt.

He angled his head, studying her. "Church work doesn't keep you busy enough?"

"I'm guessing you must be tired of doing solo dish duty. You going to turn me down?"

"You guess right." He pointed past the casual dining room to a swinging door. "Kitchen's this way."

Once inside, Katherine began rinsing the dishes he carried from the table. It was a cozy kitchen, warmed by lots of distressed pine and welcoming framed homilies. The wallpaper was a diminutive plaid, the colors mild and unobtrusive. Obviously decorated by a caring woman who had seen this charming room as the heart of her house, it was a kitchen that cried out for a happy family.

Michael began stacking the rinsed plates in the dishwasher. She reached for a sponge, but his hand closed over hers. The butterflies in her stomach morphed into hummingbirds. Yet all she could do was stare, absently noting how much larger and more tanned his hand was than hers. At five foot ten inches tall, it wasn't often she felt petite. But Michael's six-foot-four-inch frame towered above her.

And now his hand lingered on hers.

She tried to clear her suddenly clogged throat and realized she'd made a sound that resembled a bashful bullfrog.

"You don't have to do that," he was saying.

Trying again, she managed to clear her throat, yet her voice still sounded husky. "Do what?"

"Wipe down the kitchen. Despite your offer, I doubt you came here to clean house."

Katherine collected her rattled thoughts and managed an almost convincing chuckle. "I really don't mind."

He lifted his hand from hers. "But I want to know why you're here."

Show time.

Katherine smiled, then called on the Lord to guide her through this conversation. "Actually, it has to do with your kids."

He waited.

"Well...and Bible School."

His eyebrows raised in question but he didn't speak.

Still gripped by nerves, she rattled uncharacteristically. "I was going to talk with you today when you picked up the girls, but we got sidetracked, so that's why I thought I'd better come by tonight."

When she finally paused, he spoke, his tone droll. "Lots of detail, but I still don't know why you're here."

Katherine stared at him, wondering if a pair of incredible blue eyes was making her lose all sense of reason. So she took a deep breath. "You see, we have a special evening on Friday night for the vacation Bible School kids and their parents. It's pretty informal, but the kids always love it."

"I think I've made it clear how I feel about my children attending church events. I'm allowing them to come to vacation Bible School against my better judgment. However, that's it. Nothing else."

"But this *is* part of vacation Bible School," she explained. "Everyone participates in the program, and the kids will be terribly disappointed if they can't be there."

His expression was skeptical. "Are you sure the kids know about it?"

She nodded. "It's on the church calendar, so all the members have known the schedule for some time. And we sent home a note today. It's probably with the kids' Bible stories or artwork. But we've been talking about it all week...practicing songs and skits. Annie and David definitely know. And they'll feel left out if they can't attend.''

He winced, and Katherine realized she'd hit a tender spot.

''All right—''

However, it wasn't resignation she heard in his voice, but determination.

''But this has to end. I agreed to let them go to vacation Bible School, not every event the church holds.''

Although she wanted to argue, Katherine knew she would have to take this battle step by step. This small victory was enough. For now.

Chapter Three

Since Rosewood Community Church had a two-week vacation Bible School program, they treated each week as a separate unit and had a celebratory conclusion to each week so no one would feel left out.

It wasn't an elaborate ceremony. One of the members of the congregation owned a pizza business, and he donated scores of pizza for both Friday night get-togethers. Another member brought a snow cone machine. And another a cotton-candy maker. Mothers brought cakes, cookies and every imaginable dessert. The atmosphere was festive, much like when the church held its autumn carnival.

And the kids loved every moment.

Including the Carlson kids. David took one look at the endless tables of pizza and went into pepperoni frenzy. The more delicate Annie was intrigued by the intricate webs of cotton candy.

Michael watched them both, feeling them being sucked deeper into the church. As he did, he experienced a familiar pang, one he'd never completely left behind. A pang that reminded him that he had once had a church home, as well. One he valued. One he missed.

But he couldn't just forget what had happened. And he certainly couldn't forgive.

Katherine was making her way across the room, stopping to speak to nearly everyone—but then, as minister, she knew all the members. In fact, it was her job to round up those who had strayed from the flock.

But he was no lost lamb.

Michael approached his son. "Why don't we get a table?"

David studied his overloaded plate. "Think I have enough to start with?"

"And finish," Michael agreed.

"We have to get some lemonade, too," David insisted. "And cotton candy, and—"

"Let's start with the pizza, okay, bud? I'll grab the drinks, if you'll find your sister and pick out a table. She'll probably want to sit with Tessa."

"Okay. But Tessa's gonna sit with her family," David told him, before heading toward the sea of tables.

Michael joined the growing line of people waiting for punch and lemonade. It took some time to collect the drinks. When he looked for David and Annie, he didn't see them at first.

Then he spotted his daughter's luminescent face— as she gazed in admiration at Katherine. Katherine, too, was animated, laughing with the children.

Why was it that every time he turned around, she seemed to be there—and looking so remarkably attractive? She stood out among the other women like a brightly colored robin surrounded by wrens. Perhaps it wasn't a fair comparison, but just her energy alone radiated an appealing aura. Pity she was a linchpin in the church—

The thought brought him to a sudden and complete stop. He hadn't believed he was ready to feel any serious attraction to another woman.

Michael forced himself to move forward, to regain his steadiness. As he reached the table, another wave of laughter erupted. His children seemed equally charmed by Katherine. He had to admit he couldn't remember ever seeing them laugh so much.

Annie spotted him first. "Daddy!"

David was only a beat behind. "Over here, Daddy!"

Since the children sat on each side of Katherine, that left the spot directly across from her at the four-person table.

Katherine reached over, helping him unload the drinks from his tray. The automatic gesture surprised him. He had become accustomed to doing things on his own with his children.

He was even more surprised when David pushed over a plate filled with Michael's favorite—combo pizza.

"You're lucky, Mr. Carlson, the combo goes pretty fast because we have mostly cheese and pepperoni for the kids," Katherine said with a smile.

"It's 'Michael,'" he told her, remembering her insistence that he call her Katherine.

Her eyes warmed in a way that made his insides do somersaults. "Michael."

It seemed ridiculous that in the noisy, crowded

room he suddenly had the sense that there were only the two of them, sharing an unnamed tension, an unfathomable connection.

"Aren't you going to eat your pizza?" David asked.

Pulling his gaze from Katherine, he turned to his son. "I sure am. Thanks for getting mine." He was touched that his son had been so thoughtful.

"It was Katherine's idea," David told him without hesitation, digging back into his own pizza.

Michael met her eyes.

She shrugged. "No point in your fetching the drinks, then having to fend for yourself in the pizza line."

Still it was a thoughtful gesture, Michael acknowledged to himself. So, she was beautiful *and* thoughtful.

Katherine stood to hug one of the elderly members of the congregation, making the woman beam with pleasure. Michael couldn't deny that her behavior was a good example for the kids. They both looked so relaxed, so happy. Katherine was right. This had been a good experience for them.

And that thought ran riot.

Michael slammed on his mental brakes. He couldn't allow himself to believe she was right. Then, he might be duped into permitting his children to make the same mistake he had, to trust as he had—to be betrayed, as well.

Just then, Katherine met his gaze, her own urging him to join in the fun his children were having.

It was difficult, considering the proximity, for Michael to avoid her gaze. It was equally difficult to remain stern, when Katherine kept his children in stitches.

She was explaining anchovies to David, and the expressions on both their faces had even Michael fighting a chuckle.

"Tell you what, David," Katherine said with a laugh. "We'll have pizza again, my treat, and I'll find the squishiest, saltiest little fishes in town."

"Ick," Annie added with a shudder.

"No one *has* to eat them," Katherine told her with a smile. "But David *wants* to taste anchovies."

David grinned. "Neat!"

Michael rolled his eyes. This was his child? The one who wouldn't try most foods unless coerced? And, he realized, Katherine had just managed to insert another invitation into the conversation.

Then her laughing eyes met his. "So, are you an anchovies man?"

Michael realized he hadn't tasted anchovies in years because Ruth hadn't liked them. "Actually," he admitted, "I love them."

"You eat squishy fishes, Daddy?" Annie asked with a mixture of horror and admiration.

"Yeah, I'm pretty tough, sweetheart."

Katherine's laugh bounced around him. "A real macho man."

Her spirit, at once compassionate and uplifting, touched him. And he found himself reluctantly grinning.

Katherine's and Michael's gazes met, their laughter erupting simultaneously.

Unperturbed, David shook his head and attacked another piece of pizza. Annie chose the same moment to try her cotton candy. Clearly they were unimpressed.

This time, amusement and instant understanding bloomed in the glance between Katherine and Michael. It was a family sort of moment—the kind parents often shared with their children.

And that didn't seem right, Michael realized, not with a preacher.

Katherine was urging Annie to tell him about her participation in the art project.

Delighted with the attention, Annie told him about being Katherine's helper and how the teacher had praised her work. The mood lightened with her recitation.

After polishing off their pizza, Katherine gestured toward the game setup that lined two of the long walls in the church hall. "We consider this sort of a carnival preview, for the one we hold in the fall. There's a ring toss and apple bob, that sort of thing. They're simple but fun games."

"Can we do that one?" Annie pointed to a group that was holding balloons beneath their chins. The object was to pass the balloon on to the next person without using any hands. The entire group was laughing loudly at the antics the game demanded.

Michael wanted to refuse, to wind up the evening. But Annie was jumping from foot to foot, tugging on his hand. It simply wasn't possible to crush her excitement. As least, it wasn't in Michael to do so.

So he and Katherine walked with the children over to the balloon relay. The players greeted Katherine warmly, obviously fond of their minister.

The relay was popular, eliciting bursts of unrestrained laughter and much good-natured teasing. The balloons slipped as they were passed, some squeaking, some drifting to the floor.

Annie and David giggled with delight as they managed to successfully relay their balloon. Michael cheered their accomplishment, then started to turn away.

"No Daddy! You have to play, too!" Annie exclaimed.

"Yeah, Daddy!" David chimed in.

"I'm too tall," Michael protested, giving Annie a hug.

"You can play with Katherine. She's tall enough," David told him.

"Yes, Katherine!" Annie cried.

Michael shook his head, but to his surprise, Katherine was smiling gamely.

"I'm willing if you are," she said. "And I think I'm tall enough."

She was, Michael realized. His wife Ruth had been a petite woman. Katherine was very different, tall and willowy.

Dismissing that thought, he wanted to dismiss the game as well, but his children were begging him to participate.

"Then our team will have enough points to get a prize!" David told him.

Michael glanced at Katherine in question.

"The prizes are small—puzzles, comic books, bubbles—that sort of thing," she explained. Then she ruffled David's hair. "But I was hoping to get enough points for bubbles. I blow killer bubbles."

"Then, you hafta play, Daddy!" Annie responded.

Realizing he was outnumbered, Michael decided it

was time to give in gracefully. "It probably won't kill me."

"Now, that's the kind of enthusiasm that lights up the night," Katherine responded wryly.

Again her humor was infectious, and Michael took his place in the relay line. In moments he held a neon-orange balloon beneath his chin, wondering if he had completely lost his mind. But with his children jumping up and down in excitement, he turned to Katherine, to pass the balloon. To end the game, the silliness.

Then she was beside him, her face lifted up toward his to allow the balloon to slide beneath her jaw. She *was* tall, Michael acknowledged. It was as though her entire body was a tall challenge, one now only inches from his own.

Trying to ignore that fact, he scrunched the balloon more firmly and angled his head to pass it to Katherine. Obligingly, she tipped her head to one side to facilitate the relay. But it wasn't as easy as it looked.

Not without touching each other.

And Michael was determined to prevent that at all costs. Katherine was doing her part to remain at a discreet distance, as well. Consequently the balloon wasn't going anywhere.

Feeling like a fool, Michael moved a bit closer, tipping his head the other way. Rolling the balloon closer to her, he had just about completed the relay when their cheeks grazed.

For a moment they both froze.

Michael's gaze flew to meet hers. And he read the matching awareness in her expression.

"Don't drop the balloon, Daddy!" David yelled.

"Move closer!" Annie shouted.

Michael couldn't have moved closer if jet-propelled. But his children's voices brought him out of the frozen tableau. Carefully, he moved back, allowing Katherine to capture the balloon.

She held up the balloon in victory as she turned away from Michael.

For an instant he was disappointed, wondering what he might have seen in her expression. Just as suddenly, he realized he didn't dare find out.

Michael soon learned that he didn't have time to worry or wonder. His children surrounded Katherine, dragging her to the next game.

In a short time they splashed through the apple bob, laughed through the ring toss, and quick-stepped past the games of twister.

Then Annie begged for face painting, and Michael tried not to look pained. His youngest could play at that for hours.

To his surprise, Katherine's expression softened. "Why don't we give the boys a break? They probably have some he-man stuff to do. I'll take you to the face painting."

Annie clapped her hands. "Are you going to get your face painted, too?"

Michael grinned at the prospect, but Katherine surprised him again. "I'll give it a shot. I've always thought a butterfly resting on my cheek might be nice."

It probably would be, Michael realized. The instant he had that thought he remembered the feel of her cheek against his. Then she was walking away, Annie's small hand in hers.

David tugged at his jacket. "Can I have some more pizza?"

"Aren't you about to blow up?"

David shook his head. "Uh-uh. I love pizza. 'Sides, you didn't eat very much."

No, because he'd been too aware of Katherine.

"You're right, David, let's see if we can rustle up a few more pieces."

"Maybe they even have some with green stuff on it."

Michael laughed at his son's description of combo pizza. "Now, that sounds appetizing. Tell you what, I'll even eat plain."

"Not me," David announced, never one to vacillate. "I want pepperoni."

"A man who knows his own mind," Michael murmured, leading his son back to the pizza tables. *Just like his father.*

Annie's expressive eyes grew even larger as she watched the woman create a butterfly on Katherine's cheek.

"Ooh, purple!" Annie murmured, totally intrigued by an adult willing to have her face painted.

"And pink, too, I hope," Katherine replied, winking at Annie.

"Absolutely," the face painter told her, and then grinned mischievously. "I could paint a hummingbird on the other cheek."

Katherine kept her own grin in check. "I think I'll go with just the butterfly for now."

"It looks pretty," Annie told her softly. "Like magic."

At her words, Katherine imagined silvery unicorns and soft swirls of girlish pink. And she could picture

Annie deep in their midst. "I bet you have a pink room."

"Yes. My mommy fixed it for me. She was always making stuff for me."

Katherine sensed the depth of this child's loss. "I'm sure it's real pretty, sweetie."

"It is. Can you come see it and play with me?"

Incredibly touched, Katherine felt herself melt. What a precious child Annie was. "We'll have to see, okay?"

"Okay. Do we match now?"

The face painter handed them each a small mirror. "See for yourselves."

Katherine and Annie studied their reflections, then turned to each other with a grin. "Matched," they said in unison, looking at the identical butterflies on their cheeks.

Annie had requested matching designs, and Katherine had seen no reason to disagree. Briefly she wondered if this was how most mothers felt with their daughters—sharing little things, taking joy in something as simple as face painting. Then Annie reached up to hug her, and Katherine knew it must be true.

As they left the face-painting area, Annie spotted her father and brother.

Michael had noticed Katherine and Annie, as well, walking hand in hand, sharing smiles and secrets. When they neared, he studied them in surprise. He hadn't really expected Katherine to allow her face to be painted. But she was nonchalant about the butterfly. Annie, however, was excited, her blue eyes shining. And he could see that his daughter was equally captivated by Katherine herself.

Taken aback, Michael wondered how this had happened so quickly. Only days ago they hadn't even met Katherine. Now both his children were involved with church activities, something he had sworn wouldn't happen. And he was having thoughts he hadn't experienced since Ruth died. Thoughts about a minister. Thoughts that had to end now.

Chapter Four

Despite the warmth of early summer, the grasses and foliage surrounding Rosewood remained vibrantly green. Not the blue-green of drier western climates, but a lush, fertile green. Sturdy native flowers that had survived beyond spring added luscious color.

Katherine took in the surroundings she enjoyed so much, gently tugging at her dog's leash to guide him away from some thorny-looking weeds. "Snowy, those weeds are taller than you are."

Leaning over, Katherine petted him affectionately. He was her family, and her most consistent companion. There hadn't been a steady man in her life since shortly after college. Oh, men admired the dedication of her calling and what they guessed was her purity of heart.

But they didn't want to date her.

At least, not in what she considered the normal fashion. True, she had the occasional date. But most men made it clear she was a woman they respected, not one with whom they wanted to become involved.

Katherine had grown to recognize the look, one that said, *admire but don't touch.*

She was accustomed to how men reacted to her profession, but she still longed for that one special, different man. Her past should have told her a relationship wasn't possible, that no man could take the pressure of a wife who was also a minister. But one persistent niggle of hope continued to hang on, like a weed in an immaculate rose garden refusing to die no matter how often she tried to yank it out, stomp on it, even bury it.

Katherine tried not to think of herself as lonely. She had plenty of friends and the fellowship of her congregation, and they were extremely important to her. But when there was no one special in her life, no one who shared her dreams, no one with whom she expected to share her future, it was hard to dispel the loneliness. And it was equally difficult to still the longing.

Glancing down the road that seemed to stretch forever in the flat plain, Katherine spotted a bright red convertible Mustang approaching. And she felt a smile erupting.

The car skidded to a halt, and the driver tooted out a friendly greeting on the horn. "What are you doing out here in the middle of nowhere?" Cindy Thompson asked, tossing back her flame-colored hair. "Hop in and I'll buy you a soda, maybe even a root beer float."

"I've got Snowy," Katherine replied, not certain she was ready to give up her solitary walk.

"We'll get him a milk bone," Cindy replied without concern for the immaculate car interior. "Besides, I met a man."

Katherine's grin grew, suffusing her face. "You say that like it's new."

Cindy didn't take offense. "So, don't you want to hear about him?"

Katherine picked up her dog, deposited him in the backseat, and then hopped inside. "I'm all ears."

As they drove down the road, Cindy described her new and, as always, temporary Mr. Right.

Katherine listened patiently, and Cindy finally paused. "So what do you think?"

"I think I don't know much about him other than his looks."

"Katherine, I barely met him. I don't know his life history yet!"

Katherine smiled gently at her best friend, one of the few people in the small town who viewed her strictly as a friend, rather than a minister. But they went back a long way to the time when they'd both lived in Houston. In fact, when Cindy had needed to escape her big city life, she'd chosen to relocate in Rosewood because of their friendship. Cindy had never stood on ceremony with her, and Katherine appreciated every irreverent bone in her body. Also, she was aware of her friend's painful past, one she disguised with humor and outlandish behavior.

Years before, Cindy had fallen hopelessly in love with Flynn Mallory. But he had chosen Cindy's sister over her. Cindy had hoped her feelings for Flynn would fade. When they hadn't, she'd fled Houston, moving to Rosewood where she could be near her best friend. But neither time nor distance could obliterate that love. And since her parents had died, she had no other family with which to fill her life. "I didn't mean to criticize."

Cindy sighed. "I know my track record isn't good, but I also know my prince is out there. I just have to keep looking. Maybe from here to Kalamazoo, but I'm going to find him."

"Tenacity is a good quality."

Cindy threw back her head, a gust of laughter combining with the wind that skimmed over the open top of the car. "That's subtle!"

Sheepishly, Katherine grinned. "I didn't mean it quite that way."

"Pshaw," Cindy retorted. "At least I'm still looking. I haven't seen you dating anyone lately."

Katherine couldn't contain a grimace. Cindy was right on target.

"You'll meet someone."

Katherine didn't reply.

Cindy jerked her attention from the road, staring at her friend. "You *have* met someone! Who? Details! I want details!"

But Katherine hesitated. "It's not what you think. He's the father of one of the children in vacation Bible School."

Exasperated, Cindy glanced back at her. "And that makes him unacceptable, why?"

"It's more complicated than that." Briefly Katherine outlined their meeting and her subsequent discovery of Michael's feelings.

Cindy gave a low whistle. "Whew. That's tough. You can see why he's all closed off. Losing his wife and having two little kids to raise on his own."

"Of course. But he's turned his back on the Lord."

"And who better to set him in the right direction, Katherine?"

"I know it's my job—"

"It's not just your job, Katherine. It's who you are. Wouldn't you want to help him even if you weren't attracted to him?"

"Of course!"

"Then, what's the problem?"

Katherine stared straight ahead, but her composure slipped a bit. "The first time I saw him I was immediately attracted to him, which appalled me since he had three children with him and I guessed he was married. And now that I know how he feels about his faith, I'm even more disturbed to find that I'm still thinking about him in more than a spiritual way. Perhaps I should be listening to my initial feeling of alarm. Maybe it's the Lord's way of telling me that Michael is not someone I should be attracted to."

"And maybe He's telling you that this is a very special man, who needs you in more ways than you've considered."

Reluctantly Katherine turned and met her friend's gaze. Despite Cindy's frivolous appearance, her roots were grounded. "You really think so?"

"Katherine, let yourself be both a minister and a woman. You'll know which direction the Lord wants you to take. Don't just assume it's either–or. Perhaps this is a dual role."

It wasn't something Katherine had considered. For such a long time now she had stood on the outside of the relationship circle. Could it be that that was changing?

The following morning Katherine stood inside the sanctuary, glancing around at the church she loved. It was something she did early on Sunday mornings. It was a way to seek the quiet, reestablish her connection to the congregation. And today she felt a special need for that.

As was her custom, immediately before services began she slipped away to pray. And the Carlsons entered into her prayer.

When she looked up again, she was surprised to see Pastor James McPherson, the wise and Godly man with whom she had interned after seminary. As her mentor, he had guided her throughout her ministerial career.

"James! What a wonderful surprise! Is Jean with you?"

"She stopped at the nursery. You know how my wife is about babies."

That she did. James's kind and gentle wife would have a dozen babies if she could. So far they'd been blessed with only two boys. "I know they'll welcome an extra pair of arms. You should have told me you were coming to Rosewood."

"It was just an impulse. Classes are out this week at the seminary. Jean and I decided to take advantage of the break, and the boys were thrilled about a trip. Besides, it's been too long since we've seen you."

Touched by his words, her smile wobbled a bit. "It's so good to see you."

James angled his head, studying her. "Is anything wrong?"

"Not wrong, just a little heavier burden than usual."

"You know we're only two hours away, Katherine. And you can call on us anytime for help. That's what friends are for."

He and Jean were that and more. His mentoring had grounded her ministerial career, given her the direction she'd needed. "I know. But this is one problem I'm afraid I'll have to deal with on my own."

Again he searched her expression. "You know best. But don't forget we're always available."

"I'm counting on it," she replied.

He glanced at the people who had begun filing inside. "We'll talk more after the service. I'd better find a seat."

Katherine nodded, taking her place on the dais.

The pews filled rapidly even though it was early summer, a time when attendance typically dipped. Katherine found herself watching for the Carlsons, wondering if Michael Carlson could possibly have begun to relent. Even though she guessed it was far too soon for that to happen, she was disappointed that he and his family were absent.

Silly, she knew. Michael Carlson had been adamantly clear about his feelings. Still, she had hoped. She knew the Lord was working on him. But He possessed far more patience than she did.

Even though her sermon went well and almost everyone gathered on the lawns afterward for their Sunday picnic, Katherine couldn't lose her nagging feeling about the Carlsons. She wondered if Annie and David had asked to attend the picnic, if they were disappointed at not being allowed to come.

Despite her concern, she was able to interact with James, Jean and the church members, to join in the children's laughter as they romped with one another, and to be charmed by the babies.

It was one of those picture-perfect days. But Katherine couldn't fully appreciate its beauty. Tomorrow was the beginning of the second and last week of vacation Bible School. If she didn't convince Michael to allow his children to attend church beyond the week, she might never see them—or him—again.

On Monday afternoon, Michael approached the room where Annie's vacation Bible School class was held. But his feet dragged a bit as he approached. Glancing at the ceiling of the educational building, he frowned. The water stains that bled through the paint were a sign of trouble. Coupled with the antiquated wiring system, a leaky roof could cause serious trouble. And from what he'd seen of the electrical system, it could well be already compromised. Which meant the building's structural integrity might also be compromised.

Then he shook his head at the train of thought— dodging reality for his own comfort zone of contracting problems. What did they matter?

What bothered him was Katherine. He was pretty sure she would be at the door of the classroom, as she had been every day. On the previous occasions, however, he hadn't just spent two days thinking about her.

But since Friday night, she had crept relentlessly into his thoughts. It was hard to shake the image of her making his kids laugh and forget the gloom they'd been living with. It was equally easy to remember Katherine hugging Annie, then turning around to present their matching butterflies. It was an unexpected moment of whimsy, a breath of something so fresh he hadn't known what to say.

And he still didn't.

But when he arrived at the classroom, Katherine wore her usual smile. So perhaps she hadn't attached any special significance to the evening.

Not certain whether to be relieved or disappointed, he collected backpacks and children. Ready to leave, he saw David flying down the hall toward him.

"Aren't you supposed to wait until I get to your room?" Michael asked him, corralling the youthful bundle of energy.

"Teacher said it was okay when I saw you right here," David explained.

Coming up behind him with Annie in hand, Katherine smiled. "His class and ours played outside together today. His teacher knows that Annie's his sister."

With all the frightening things happening to children in the news, Michael didn't approve of the practice. "Next time wait, young man."

Recognizing the serious tone in his father's voice, David sobered a bit. "Okay, Daddy."

Michael draped one hand over his son's shoulder. "We'd better get going."

"Are we still having a barbecue?" David asked anxiously. "You don't have to work late again, do you?"

"Nope. We're having my world-famous hamburgers."

"It's the only thing he really knows how to cook," David told Katherine candidly.

"I'm sure that's not true," Katherine replied.

"Afraid he's right," Michael conceded ruefully.

But Katherine didn't respond in the sympathetic tones he had expected.

Instead, she burst into laughter. "Sorry," she finally managed to say. "Most men aren't usually so honest."

"My daddy's always honest," Annie told her, forever the loyal child.

"Oh, I'm sure he is," Katherine responded. "And I bet he's a champion hamburger cooker."

"He is," Annie agreed. Then her small face lit up. "Why don't you come taste?" She turned to her father. "Katherine can come eat hamburgers with us, can't she, Daddy?"

And how was he supposed to say no?

Especially when David chimed in. "Yeah, Daddy. She could see you're the best!"

Katherine looked a bit embarrassed, but she smiled at the children. "I don't want to intrude."

"She wouldn't be 'truding, would she, Daddy?" Annie questioned.

Michael stared helplessly at his daughter, who was positioned between them, looking from one uncomfortable adult to the other.

"Of c-course not," Michael stammered.

"If you're sure," Katherine murmured.

"We're sure," David answered for him. "Can you bring dessert?"

Michael rolled his eyes in embarrassment, but Katherine was laughing again. "Two honest men in the Carlson family! I'd be happy to, David."

"It's just that Daddy's not so good on dessert," Annie whispered to her.

Katherine hugged her lightly. "It'll give me something to do. Dessert's my thing."

"We like lots," David told her.

Michael glanced down at his son, hoping the boy could read the admonishment in his expression. "Let's remember our manners, David."

"But I thought she'd wanna know," David protested.

Tactfully, Katherine bit her lip and refrained from either laughter or a defense for his forthright child.

"We'll eat around seven," Michael told her. "I think you know the address."

A bit of color crept into her cheeks. It surprised him. He didn't think a direct, candid woman like Katherine would blush.

She cleared her throat. "Right, I do. I'll be there with bells on."

"And dessert," David reminded her.

Unable to resist the laughter lurking in Katherine's eyes, Michael repeated David's words. "Lots."

Her laughter spilled out. David, Annie and Tessa joined her.

Funny. He'd just been hog-tied into inviting the woman to dinner, and yet it was difficult to remain provoked. Belatedly Michael remembered that Katherine was the reason he now stood in the church hall. And he told himself it would be easy to regain his annoyance. Then his glance strayed back to Katherine and somehow he doubted his own resolve.

The summer days were long, spilling sunshine past the huge trees in Michael's yard. Spreading branches provided canopies of shade while bougainvillea crept across the fence and trailed over an ancient arbor.

The yard was old and somewhat softened, like the house, a weathered Cape Cod that boasted a wide porch running around the entire perimeter.

Katherine thought the home was filled with charm and character. She believed that houses, like people, were more interesting with a bit of age. Personality didn't develop overnight, and this one had mellowed delightfully over the years.

Michael had greeted her with reserve, and Katherine keenly felt her occupation standing between them. It was a barrier neither could ignore. But for the children's sake, Katherine was determined to be upbeat. She sensed they needed more laughter. And that was something she could provide, regardless of Michael's resolve.

Katherine wrapped the last ear of corn in aluminum foil and added it to the platter. "This should be yummy."

"I like stuff cooked outside," Annie agreed.

"Me, too." As she took a deep breath of the fragrant air, the smell of mesquite chips lured her to the grill.

With Annie at her side, together they handed the corn to Michael. While he hadn't requested that she bring a vegetable, Katherine had thought the kids might enjoy it.

Michael eyed the corn on the cob dubiously. "You and I will probably be the only ones to eat it, but we can toss it on the grill."

"I'll eat some, Daddy," Annie insisted.

Katherine shared a smile with her, realizing that the child had a special gift for always wanting others to feel happy. It was remarkable for one so young.

"Should we set the table?" Katherine asked David and Annie.

"Sure," they replied in unison.

Michael's eyebrows rose. "That's a first."

"Usually we take turns," David explained.

"And they don't volunteer," Michael added.

Hearing this, Katherine decided to make a game of

the chore. "How about a contest? Let's divide the table in half." With her hand she drew an imaginary line down the middle of the tablecloth. "You each have half a table to decorate."

"Decorate?" Annie asked. "You mean like Christmas?"

"Not exactly, sweetie, but something like that. I'll leave it to your imaginations. You have plates, napkins, glasses and silverware to work with."

"Is that all?" David asked.

She thought for a moment. "I guess not. You can use other things, too, but nothing too big or too messy."

Together the three of them carried the dinnerware from the kitchen. A second and then third trip yielded all the condiments and hamburger buns. Another trip brought lemonade and chips. Katherine noticed that Michael remained at the grill, as though using it to keep the distance between them.

Then the children scattered to collect what they were using for the table-decorating contest.

"Don't look!" David and Annie cried as they brought their loot back to the table.

Obligingly, Katherine sat in one of the overstuffed lawn chairs away from the table. And she couldn't help noticing that Michael didn't move from his spot at the grill. Katherine wondered if he intended to spend the evening there, perhaps munching on his burger from a safe distance.

As she watched him, he lifted his gaze, almost as though he sensed her eyes on him. Again that nameless tension hung in the air. Wildly attracted to him, she wondered if the feeling was one-sided. But if so, why did the pressure seem to radiate between them?

Katherine smiled a trifle tenuously, wishing she could ban her uncharacteristic uncertainty. But his gaze remained thoughtful, neither antagonistic nor welcoming.

She was a threat, Katherine realized, and one he wasn't certain how to banish. When he looked at her, she guessed, he must be constantly reminded of the church, and the loss that drove him from it. In a purely feminine fashion, she wondered if he saw more...wanted more.

The minutes passed and the hamburgers cooked, their smell a tantalizing aroma that brought all of Katherine's hunger buds to life, despite her nerves.

"Burgers are done," Michael announced finally and the children ran toward him. "Hope you guys remembered the mustard."

"And pickles," Annie replied happily. "And cheese, too!"

He smiled fondly at his youngest. "Good." Then he glanced at Katherine. "Why don't you two escort our guest to the table."

"Okay, Daddy," Annie replied.

"Then you guys have to judge the table," David insisted. "Before we eat."

Michael raised his brows at Katherine. "Another first."

But he walked over to the table with his children. Initially, surprise held him in silence. He had seen the children playing by the table, but he hadn't guessed they would glean so much from Katherine's suggestion.

"Whose side do you like?" David demanded.

"Oh, my," Katherine murmured.

Michael stepped closer to the table that now resembled a fantasyland that could only have been dreamed up by children.

David's side looked as though it had been plucked from a miniature army bivouac. Tiny soldiers guarded each plate, reinforced by a row of tanks. A helicopter had landed amidst the napkins, while silverware resembled a bridge, crossed by foot soldiers.

And Annie's side was as whimsical as David's was realistic. Barbie, Ken and their friends sat by each plate. Barbie's swimming pool and slide looked poised for a party. On each plate either a tiny hat or equally minuscule pair of shoes decorated the center. Annie had draped her toy pink feather boa atop her makeshift centerpiece, a final piece of whimsy.

How had so much creativity flowed from his children?

As he continued to stand mute, Katherine draped her hands over their shoulders. "This is wonderful!" She gazed at the table again, then emitted a low whistle. "Just wonderful. Both sides. I knew you'd both do a fabulous job, but this is even better than I expected. It's Barbie World And G.I. Joe Land!"

David and Annie both grinned at the praise, then turned to their father.

"What do you think, Daddy?"

Jerked from his startled silence, Michael crouched down between his children. "It *is* wonderful—just like you guys."

Annie looped her arms around his neck. "Thanks, Daddy."

"But who won?" David asked.

"Both of you," he replied. "You made something fabulous and you worked together to do it. And now we have a beautiful table to sit down to. We're all winners.''

"But you weren't in the contest," David pointed out practically.

"Of course he was," Katherine inserted gently. "As your father, he's always with you in everything you do, cheering you on, feeling what you feel. And he's always on both your sides."

"I like it that we both win," Annie replied generously.

"Yeah, it's okay," David agreed.

Michael watched Katherine's interaction with his children and again he wondered, How was it she managed to say just the right thing? As remarkable was his children's reaction. Perhaps they were simply craving a woman's attention. But if he were honest, he had to admit Mrs. Goode hadn't elicited the same response.

"Then, if your dad's ready, maybe he'll let us dig into those burgers," Katherine suggested, lightening the mood.

"Yeah, burgers!" David replied. "My daddy makes the best."

"It's one of those macho guy things," Katherine confided to him.

"But girls eat 'em, too, don't they, Katherine?" Annie asked seriously, her hand poised above the buns, hesitating.

"We *devour* them," Katherine replied, pretending to reach out and tickle her.

Annie giggled.

The more practical David trotted back to the grill, retrieving the plate that held the burgers.

"They smell heavenly," Katherine declared.

Michael searched for a hidden meaning to that particular description, but she was helping the kids put the plate on the table, not waiting for a reply from him.

When Michael took his seat, he saw Katherine glance at him in question. No doubt she wondered if he planned to say a blessing over the food. Deliberately he set his mouth in a thin line. Not anymore.

Instead, he reached for the hamburger platter. To his surprise, Katherine assisted him, even though her eyes told him she thought the food should be blessed first.

He offered the first burger to her, and soon every gooey condiment was opened and being poured. Katherine capitulated easily when Annie suggested they build identical burgers. She only flinched mildly when Annie heavily covered both buns with sliced sour pickles, and gamely followed suit.

Michael found himself enjoying the sight.

"I almost forgot the corn!" Katherine exclaimed, popping up from the table. Pulling on his chef mitts, she retrieved the corn from the grill. "Any takers?" she asked, returning to the table.

"Me!" David shouted.

"Me!" Annie chimed in.

Michael guessed they would agree to anything she suggested. But he still didn't think his son would actually eat the corn.

Katherine peeled away the aluminum foil, then buttered each ear. "It's best when it's almost dripping butter," she told them seriously.

"Sold me," Michael said, not wanting her to feel too rebuffed when the kids didn't dive in.

She smiled. "I love fresh corn. When I was grow-

ing up, we often got donations of corn that had just
been picked.''

"Donations?'' Michael asked.

For a moment she looked uncomfortable. Then she
reached for the saltshaker. ''My mother was involved
in a lot of charitable projects, and people often gave
us the overage from their gardens. And they always
brought some for my family, too.''

"Do you have a big family?'' Annie asked.

Katherine shook her head. ''Just my mom and
dad.''

"No brothers?'' Annie asked with great concern,
as though this were a terrible and unjust misfortune.

"Afraid not,'' Katherine replied. ''You're lucky to
have each other.''

An only child, Michael thought. Yet she seemed
overly generous, not at all like the stereotypical only
child.

But his attention was pulled away from her when
he saw his son take a bite of corn. Then another. And
another.

Katherine didn't look triumphant, only pleased. ''A
friend gave me the corn. And it was just picked today.''

Michael took a bite, too. Sweet and moist, it was
the best corn he'd tasted in longer than he could remember. ''Can't beat fresh. Thanks for bringing it. I
can't believe David's not only eating a vegetable—
he volunteered.''

"It's just something different,'' she dismissed with
good grace.

They all polished off the delicious ears of sweet
corn, chins dribbling with butter and rivulets of corn
juice.

Michael reached over to wipe David's chin. "And I *really* can't believe you're on your second ear."

"This doesn't *taste* like vegetables," David explained. "It tastes *good.*"

Katherine laughed. "That's how I feel about grilled squash."

"Ick," David replied without hesitation. "Nothing you can do to squash would make it taste good."

"I thought so, too," she agreed. "Then I had some on a grilled shish kebab."

"What's a shishbob?" Annie asked.

"Lots of yummy stuff on a stick."

"Will you make it for us sometime?"

Michael cleared his throat. "Annie, you don't invite other people to cook for you."

Katherine smiled diplomatically. "My fault again, I'm afraid. Tell you what, if you decide you'd like 'shishbobs' for dinner one night, I'll be happy to cook."

Michael studied her face, wondering at hidden motives. They were either nonexistent or he was too out of practice to tell. That or she was so consumed with bringing his family back to church that she hid her true motive well. And it was that final thought that bothered him.

But before he could think of a way out of this newest invitation, David spoke. "Can we have dessert now? What'd you bring?"

"Actually, I brought two things. I wasn't sure what you'd like so there's a choice."

"You shouldn't have gone to so much trouble," Michael protested, knowing this treatment might spoil his children, actually get them used to edible food.

"It wasn't any trouble," Katherine replied. "Although I don't do a lot of cooking, I enjoy it. But I'm always putting a twist on standard recipes. When I was a kid I tried everything. For a while I went through a stage where I tinted everything I cooked with food color. My father was a very patient soul, but even he had a hard time going through the blue food stage.''

"Blue?" the kids asked together, fascinated.

Katherine met Michael's eyes, sharing his amusement. "And I wouldn't recommend it—nothing looks like it would taste too good in blue. Trust me.''

"What else did you make?" David asked.

"Well…I think I tried every single flavor of jelly mixed with every imaginable thing I could find in the fridge.''

"Your mom didn't mind?" Annie questioned.

For a moment a strange, almost unhappy look passed over Katherine's face. Michael wondered why.

"My mom wasn't into cooking much, so she didn't mind my experiments.''

"My mommy was a good cook," Annie told her.

"I'm sure she was, sweetie. I bet she was the best.''

After she spoke, Katherine met Michael's eyes, and he saw the compassion there. Michael again felt the sense of loss his family continued to endure. Yet, somehow, with Katherine seated across from him, it didn't seem so bad.

"Why don't we get the dessert?" Katherine suggested. "I could use two helpers.''

Annie and David immediately rose, scampering beside her as they headed back into the kitchen.

Michael couldn't still his sense of amazement at how completely his children seemed to accept Katherine. She wasn't anything like their mother, yet they seemed drawn to her shelter much like baby birds to their nest.

Soon the trio returned from the house, each carrying something.

"We're doing s'mores, Daddy!" Annie announced, putting the marshmallows and chocolate bars on the table.

David plunked down the box of graham crackers and, surprisingly, a jar of chunky peanut butter.

"My little twist," Katherine explained, catching his glance resting on the peanut butter. "I love chocolate-peanut butter cups, so I thought, why not?" As she spoke, she put an elaborate glazed, fresh fruit tart in the center of the table. "And I've always loved these."

He glanced appreciatively at the exquisitely prepared dessert. "It looks delicious."

She bent a bit closer, lowering her voice. "I brought the s'mores in case the kids don't like it."

"I think they'd like anything you do," he told her truthfully.

Again, surprising him, she colored a bit, her hands suddenly nervous, fussing with the dessert plates. "I'll help the kids with the s'mores."

As she headed toward the grill, Michael found himself following. *To supervise the kids,* he rationalized.

He noticed that she had brought long metal hot dog holders with safe wooden handles. She'd thought of everything. And that bothered him. He didn't want to like her as a person. She represented the church that his children were already enjoying too much.

"Mine are almost done," Annie was saying.

"Those aren't cooked enough," David dismissed.

"You want yours charred," Katherine commented. "I like them well done, too, but they're great on the s'mores when they're just gooey like Annie's."

"So they'll work both ways," Michael told them.

"I could cook mine a little more," Annie said, not quite ready to give up her place at the grill.

"Whatever you think, princess," he told her.

"Aren't you going to cook one, Daddy?" Annie asked.

"Oh, sure. I love a good s'more." He picked up one of the roasting sticks, pushed a few marshmallows on the end and joined their circle around the grill.

When they had assembled the graham crackers, chocolate and marshmallow, Katherine gave them the option of peanut butter, as well.

Michael watched as Annie readily agreed. David was another matter. He was a member of probably one of the most minuscule groups in the world—children who don't like peanut butter.

But Katherine took it in stride. "I like s'mores both ways, regular and peanut butter. It's the differences in this world that make things interesting. Just like people."

"People?" David questioned, still not certain he wasn't being teased about his peanut butter aversion.

"Don't you know some people who aren't a lot like you?" Katherine asked.

David thought a moment. "The kids that live by the place Daddy's working on. We go there sometimes when Mrs. Goode can't watch us."

"Did you see them do anything fun while you were there?" Katherine asked, wiping marshmallow goo from her fingers.

David brightened immediately. "They hit a paper donkey that was hanging from a tree."

Katherine met Michael's gaze, and they both smiled.

"A piñata," Michael told him, remembering how all the workmen had paused to watch and grin as the children attacked the piñata, joining their laughter. He hadn't realized David would remember the moment so vividly.

"And that's different," Katherine added. "In a good way, don't you think?"

David nodded. "It looked like lots of fun."

"Maybe sometime your dad would let you and Annie have a piñata. One of the best things about the traditions of other cultures is that we can borrow some of them and make our own lives more interesting."

Michael enjoyed her analogy nearly as much as her positive outlook.

"I think my s'more needs another marshmallow," Annie announced.

Katherine reached for a roasting stick. "Let me make a few more. I like to eat the extras."

"I don't know," Michael observed. "I could skip the graham crackers and marshmallows and go straight for the chocolate."

"But then they're not s'mores, Daddy," Annie protested.

"So they're not, princess. Tell you what. I'll help Katherine make a few more marshmallows, and then you and David can both have another s'more."

"Yea!" David cheered.

He noticed that Katherine's glance slid toward him as they stood beside the grill. A breeze drifted through the trees teasing tendrils of smoke between them.

Even though the children were only across the yard, it seemed oddly as though they were alone in the approaching twilight.

Even Katherine's voice was quieter, softer. "Thank you."

"For what?"

"This evening—allowing me to enjoy your children."

He shrugged. "Just a barbecue."

"Maybe so. But I've really had a good time."

Michael wasn't ready to agree with her, to admit that it had been a pleasant evening.

In the silence Katherine fussed with the roasting stick. Suddenly she jerked one hand away. "Ouch!"

"What did you do?" he asked, setting his own roasting stick on the cart beside the grill.

"Oh it's nothing," she replied, still holding the tender spot.

Michael reached for her hand.

"It's so silly," she protested. "I shouldn't have touched the metal."

But he was already turning over her hand. "It's blistering."

To his surprise he felt a trace of trembling in the hand he held.

"I'm such a klutz," she apologized, an odd note in her voice.

He traced the outline of the burn. It wasn't serious, just a reddening of her pale skin. Her very pale skin.

Glancing up, he met her eyes, fielding the questions there, staggered by the ones forming in his own thoughts. Her lips parted in a little *O*, and he sensed trouble. Trouble in the form of a minister. An intriguing, beautiful minister. One whose hand he still held. Worse, one whose hand he wanted to continue holding.

Chapter Five

Three days later Katherine was unusually quiet. As she had been all morning and the preceding two days and nights. She couldn't stop thinking about the Carlson family. More specifically, Michael.

She thought it was telling that he hadn't picked up the children from vacation Bible School either day. But surely it was too much to imagine that he was equally uncomfortable. She doubted that he had read more into the simple touch of their hands than was warranted.

But she couldn't forget the look that passed between them.

And that had all her alarm bells clanging. Despite her longing to have a special man in her life, she knew it wasn't to be, and it certainly couldn't be Michael.

He was a father, a family man. And she knew what happened to men like that when paired with women like her. She could easily remember her own father's pain, the bewildering realization that he counted so little in his wife's estimation. It had been devastating to him. And in Katherine's opinion, he had never truly recovered.

Equally important, she couldn't ever forget Michael's spiritual needs. Needs he continued to deny. Needs that as a minister she should be concentrating on.

Instead, she was agonizing over her personal failures, her own needs. Immersed in her thoughts, she barely heard the knock on her office door.

Cindy entered, her voice equally jarring and cheering. "Well, you look like yesterday's leftovers."

"Thanks."

Cindy stepped closer. "Any special reason for the gloom and doom?"

"Just thinking."

"Morbidly, from the look of you."

Katherine grimaced. "That bad?"

"Yep." Cindy dropped into one of the chairs across from Katherine's desk. "This have anything to do with the seriously good-looking man you think you shouldn't be interested in?"

Katherine was startled into a smile. "What makes you think he's *seriously* good-looking?"

"Because I, my friend, am an optimist."

"Do you suppose that's why we're hopeless romantics?"

"No doubt," Cindy replied with an unflappable calm. "But what would you rather do? Buy a rocker, support hose and a cat in preparation for your future?"

Katherine glanced out the window that offered a wide sweeping view of the church grounds. "Snowy might not take to a cat."

"Then, what are you going to do about this man?"

"Do?" Katherine fiddled with the word in her mind as she had all morning. "He's wounded, Cindy. In so many ways."

"Then, he's lucky to have met you."

Katherine searched for any teasing in her friend's face. But she didn't see any. "I'm not so sure." Quickly she recounted the evening at Michael's house, the barbecue, her own awareness of him.

Cindy's voice was gentle. "It sounds like a really nice time."

Katherine lowered her head. "I thought so, too. But he's avoided picking up his children from vacation Bible School for two days now."

"Maybe he's just been busy, had work conflicts."

"Could be."

"But you don't think so."

"Not really. But perhaps I'm making more of it than I should. Maybe he hasn't given the evening...or me a second thought."

"Then, why is he avoiding you?"

"I keep coming round to the same point, Cindy. First I tell myself it's my imagination. Then I'm convinced that I'm failing him as a minister."

"Maybe he'll be at the picnic this afternoon."

Katherine stared again out the window. "I hope you're right. I really need some answers."

But Katherine didn't get her answers that afternoon. Or the next. Michael appeared determined to stay away. Even though she knew it wasn't sensible, she felt a familiar prick of hurt.

Yet Katherine couldn't help hoping he would accompany his children tonight to the Friday night wrap ceremony. The church had already filled with volunteers who were bringing food and supplies, setting up games and tables. Although she was surrounded by people, Katherine felt a shaft of loneliness so deep the ache resonated through her senses.

It seemed everyone was paired off or grouped into family units. However, she was expected to be a strong leader, the person with all the answers. And so she smiled, greeting people, asking all the right questions, listening as best she could.

Her gaze skipped across the crowd, though, searching. Yet she didn't see the Carlsons...no Michael. Determinedly she kept to the task at hand, making certain everything flowed smoothly.

The minutes passed, and it was nearly time for the program to begin. Children had filled the first few rows of folding chairs, waiting for their opportunity to be front and center. Tessa, was seated on the first row, precocious as always.

Someone caught Katherine's attention, and she turned away for a few moments. When she looked back, to her delighted surprise, both Annie and David were sitting with Tessa. David was speaking to another boy, but Annie waved immediately, seeking her attention.

Unable to repress her own answering grin, Katherine waved in return. Her stomach flip-flopped as she searched nonchalantly for Michael amidst the surrounding adults. At first she didn't see him, then a pair of broad shoulders and a casual pose caught her eye.

The rush of blood that warmed her face was anything but nonchalant.

But he wasn't meeting her gaze. Feeling incredibly

foolish at the snub, Katherine turned away, heading across the room to take her seat.

Within a few minutes, the program began. The children sang several songs, their enthusiasm camouflaging any forgotten words or missed notes.

Then the children chosen to recite Bible verses lined the front of the room. To Katherine's surprise, David was among the children. Immediately concerned, her eyes sought out Michael once again. What would he think of this? Would he believe she had engineered his son's inclusion in the recital?

She couldn't tell. Michael's gaze was focused on his son.

David recited a verse, his voice steady and confident. Katherine found herself smiling fondly—more so than her usual reaction to the children in the congregation.

Then she glanced again at Michael. His face was tight, his expression closed. Immediately she wondered at the pain he held deep inside, the pain that motivated each action, each decision.

The program continued, ending with a charming tune sung by all the children. Then they walked from the front of the room, dispersing to claim parents and friends.

Annie skipped toward Katherine, her eyes shining. "Hi!"

"That was wonderful!"

"Could you hear me sing?" Annie asked earnestly.

"Of course. How could I miss such a sweet voice?"

Annie beamed. "Come with me to see Daddy, okay?"

Katherine tried to think of a kind way to refuse the

request, but she couldn't crush the expectation gleaming in the child's eyes. Instead, she called on the strength of her faith, knowing it was time to step into her dual role.

David had reached Michael first, clearly seeking his father's approval. Katherine met Michael's gaze, her own beseeching him to not crush David's enthusiasm.

Michael dropped his hand on David's shoulder, a wordless gesture of approval.

And Katherine released a breath she hadn't realized she had been holding.

"Daddy, can we go to our classrooms so we can see what we made?" Annie asked, bouncing in her excitement.

"Don't you know?" he teased her gently, tapping her head.

She giggled. "Uh-huh, but you don't!"

"Good point," he conceded.

"It's just a casual walk-through," Katherine explained. "Much like open house at school. And the children can take home their art projects tonight."

Annie clapped her hands.

Michael finally met Katherine's eyes, but he disguised his thoughts well. "Then, I guess we'd better see them."

Together they headed down the hallway, Annie clutching her father's hand, urging him to walk faster. Once inside, she became a mini tour guide, making them all smile.

But it was when she reached her art project that her enthusiasm peaked. Carefully Annie picked up a small clay picture frame and handed it to her father. "It's for you, Daddy."

Taking the frame from her outstretched hands, Michael then knelt beside her. "For me, princess?"

"Yes, Daddy, to show you how much I love you. Like Jesus loves us."

Michael's throat worked, then he hugged his daughter tightly. "Thank you, baby." His voice was husky; he sounded nearly undone.

Knowing how the effort must be costing him, Katherine felt her own chest clog with emotion.

"You can put a picture in it, Daddy."

"And I think I know just whose picture," he told her, hugging her again.

"Do you really like it?"

"It's the best present I could get."

She beamed. "Then, does this mean I can come to Sunday School?"

His head jerked up, meeting Katherine's startled gaze, his own accusing. And she couldn't think of one word of explanation.

The late evening seemed empty of its earlier promise. Everything appeared dimmer, even the coffee shop in which Katherine and Michael now sat.

She was prepared to offer conciliatory words, but the waitress appeared quickly, taking their order, chatting amiably.

The coffee arrived with equal speed. Each delay dried Katherine's throat that much more. Fiddling with the cup, she added cream even though she usually drank her coffee black.

"You asked for this meeting," Michael began, his voice void of inflection.

But sensing his underlying anger, she reached inwardly for strength. "I know you were upset earlier this evening.'' Glancing up, she saw the quiet irony reflected in his eyes. She rushed to fill the tense silence. ''More than upset. But I want you to know that I had no idea Annie would ask to attend Sunday School.''

''Not even a stray suggestion?''

She couldn't miss the sarcasm in his voice, but she also couldn't rise to the challenge. Instead, she remembered the pain he harbored, the pain that had taken over his life. ''No, but it must be equally clear to you that Annie loves going to church. Most children do. We teach love and kindness. Things Annie's obviously already been taught, so it feels natural, welcoming.''

''A difficult point to argue, but you knew that. Now, what am I going to say to Annie? How am I going to tell her no?''

Katherine leaned forward, pushing aside the coffee cup. ''Does it have to be no?''

''I think I've made it clear how I feel.''

''You've told me how difficult things have been since your wife's death. Perhaps having more people to interact with can help Annie through this time.''

''Not those particular people.''

''Like me?'' she asked, unable to completely repress her hurt.

Exasperation flickered in his eyes. ''That's not what I meant. I've been honest about my feelings. Yet my children have been sucked further and further into the church.''

''Only because they want to be,'' she reminded him gently. ''I know how difficult your loss has been, but please don't punish the children because they're drawn to a healing place.''

"If God had answered our prayers, they wouldn't need healing."

Compassion filled her heart, misting her eyes. "There are many answers. Even more than all the questions we have. Please remember that, Michael. And don't make the solution more difficult than the problem."

Michael met her gaze without speaking. And Katherine knew he was battling both past and present. She could only pray that the Lord would show him the path.

An hour later, Michael kept his tread light as he walked down the dimly lit hallway. Mrs. Goode had put the kids to bed, and he didn't want to waken them. The baby-sitter had warned him again that if his hours didn't improve, she would quit. It was yet another problem to tackle, one for which he had no answer.

Luckily, Tessa's mother was still willing to pick up the kids from any activities. But he hated to depend on others. Often, he'd had to take David and Annie with him on the job when Mrs. Goode wasn't available. But it wasn't a good situation for any of them. Entering David's room, he smiled at his young soldier. Apparently David had been playing with his army toys until the moment he'd fallen asleep. He was surrounded by miniature tanks, jeeps and infantrymen.

"So the battle wore you out," Michael whispered, smoothing the hair back from David's forehead. Then he lifted the toys from the bed, soundlessly replacing them in plastic crates. Turning back to the bed he pulled the blanket up, smoothing it over bare arms.

It was remarkable how vulnerable a child looked

when sleeping. Inside him arose a fierce need to protect and love. It seemed the world was full of more pitfalls and challenges each day. How was he to shield his children from them all? Especially now that he didn't have God to count on anymore.

"Dream of better tomorrows, son," Michael whispered before retreating quietly.

Annie's room was as girlish as David's was all boy. Michael crossed the pale pink carpet to the white canopied bed, which was awash in ruffles.

He was bending to check on Annie, when her voice startled him.

"Is that you, Daddy?"

"Yes, princess. What are you doing awake?"

"I was hoping you'd come tuck me in."

He sat on the side of her bed. "You were?"

"Uh-huh. Daddy, did you really like your present?"

He flinched, grateful for the darkness that camouflaged the motion. "Yes, sweetheart, I loved it."

"Katherine said you would!"

Michael paused. "She did?"

"Uh-huh. She's so nice, Daddy. She makes me feel special."

"Special?"

"Like Mommy did."

Michael's heart stung, knowing how much his daughter needed a woman's attention, also knowing how much they both missed Ruth. Why, though, had Annie glommed on to Katherine? It frightened him to think that breaking this attachment might hurt Annie even more. "But she's not like mommy, sweetheart."

"But she makes me feel good inside, like Mommy did."

Michael sighed. "I'm glad you enjoyed your time with her."

"I'll see her some more, Daddy, when we go to Sunday School."

"Annie, I'm not sure about Sunday School."

"Then, when will I see Katherine?"

"Sweetheart, I'm not sure she has time—"

"Katherine said she'd always have time for me!" Annie wailed.

Michael strove for patience, for a way to make his daughter understand. "Grown-ups often say things like that, but—"

"She meant it, Daddy! She wouldn't lie in Jesus's house!"

Michael blinked. Of course he and Ruth had taught their children the commandments. He just hadn't expected Annie to use one in Katherine's defense. "I didn't say she lied."

"Then, you know she'll see me when we go to Sunday School."

"Annie, families go together to church."

"David wants to go, too. He really likes Katherine. He says she's funny. She made you laugh, too, Daddy."

Yes, she had. But he hadn't expected that to be another nail in his coffin. Michael made one last attempt. "What if she doesn't have time on Sunday?"

"She will," Annie replied confidently.

Michael didn't know what to tell Annie. Perhaps Katherine wouldn't have the time she'd promised. After all, a minister had obligations. And if Katherine let the relationship wither, rather than him having to force the point, maybe his daughter wouldn't be as crushed.

However, that meant allowing Annie and David to attend Sunday School. And that was only a day away. A day until he gambled with his children's lives.

Chapter Six

Harmeniah Goode was much like her name—a good woman who was a bit of a contradiction. She enjoyed her job caring for the Carlson children, but she also had responsibilities of her own, which included an ailing sister. Harmeniah was getting on in years, and the long hours were taxing.

Yet she was torn because she was genuinely fond of young David and Annie. Harmeniah had been pleased when Michael had allowed his children to attend vacation Bible School. And she'd been downright stunned when he had agreed to let them go to Sunday School. They had attended twice now. Heartened, she'd thought it was a sign that he would be spending more time with his children. But he was still working long hours. Hours Harmeniah no longer had to sacrifice.

Which was why she had called Katherine Blake. Both children had spoken of the minister continually. But that wasn't surprising to Harmeniah since she knew Pastor Blake to be a warm and personable woman.

The doorbell rang, and Harmeniah wiped her hands on her apron, rushing to open the door. "Thank you for coming."

"Certainly, Harmeniah. It sounded urgent."

"It's my sister, Evelyn. She needs to go into the hospital, Pastor."

Katherine didn't bother asking the woman to call her by her first name. She'd tried before to no avail. Harmeniah had said she was too old to change her ways. Instead, Katherine laid a comforting hand on the older woman's arm. "And you need prayer?"

"Actually I need to leave, and there's no one to watch the kids. Since I know you and the Carlson children know you, I thought maybe you could stay with them until Mr. Carlson comes home from work."

"Certainly—if you're sure it will be all right with him."

"It'll have to be," Harmeniah replied frankly. "I've warned him again and again that I can't work these long hours. And I told him about Evelyn's appointment with the specialist today. But his mind's never quite there, if you know what I mean."

Katherine drew her brows together. "Not exactly."

"His mind's always on either work or how to keep his family together."

"I'm sure it's been difficult since he lost his wife," Katherine murmured.

"But it's time he moved on," Harmeniah announced.

"Excuse me?"

"He's too young to stay married to a memory. And his kids need a mother—someone like you, Pastor."

Katherine swallowed, coughed, then swallowed again. "Excuse me?" she repeated.

"Never did understand why you aren't married, Pastor. Need to put the both of you in a bag and shake you up, see what falls out."

"That's a whimsical thought, Harmeniah, but not very practical. Besides, how do you know Mr. Carlson isn't happy as he is?"

"Does he look happy to you?" Harmeniah asked bluntly.

Katherine hesitated. He looked anything but happy. "Still…"

"You take my advice, Pastor. And don't wait until it's too late, if you know what I mean." She raised her graying eyebrows to emphasize her point. "But for right now, can you watch the kids?"

"Certainly, Harmeniah. My schedule is free tonight. Should I try to contact Michael?"

"Don't think it'll do you any good. I've been trying his mobile phone for two hours. I get a message saying it's out of area. I have to be honest with you, Pastor. Sometimes he's a lot later than he expects to be."

"Where are the children?"

"Out back. I didn't want to tell them about you until I was sure you could stay. No point in getting their hopes up in case you had other plans."

Katherine felt an unexpected flicker of something she couldn't quite define—a combination of disbelief and surprising joy. "You really think they would have been disappointed?"

Harmeniah waved one hand in dismissal. "This family needs you, Pastor, all of them."

Katherine lifted her eyes, meeting the older woman's knowing gaze.

Harmeniah untied the strings of her apron, then pulled it off. "I was just planning to get dinner started."

"I don't mind cooking."

"It's up to you, but I don't want to cause you extra work. Fact is, I never had to ask anyone for help before to do my job."

It occurred to Katherine that the woman was feeling both guilty and a bit incompetent. She shouldn't be, but there it was.

"Harmeniah, you're not asking for help in doing *your* job, you're asking help for Michael in doing *his*."

To Katherine's surprise and apparently Harmeniah's mortification, tears appeared in the older woman's eyes. "You do have a way with you, Pastor." Then, embarrassed, Harmeniah fled to the next room.

Katherine waited until she heard the other woman collect her things before entering the kitchen. "Harmeniah, perhaps you should come with me to tell the children why I'm here."

Now composed, Harmeniah nodded. "Good idea, Pastor." Not wasting another moment, she marched into the backyard. Katherine trailed behind.

"David! Annie!" the older woman called. "Come here!"

The kids ran toward them from the far end of the deep yard. When they spotted Katherine, they grinned, running even faster.

"Katherine!" they both shouted.

"Hi, guys!" Katherine greeted them.

"What're you doing here?" David asked. "Did you bring dessert?"

Katherine hooted, but Harmeniah plopped disapproving hands on both hips. "Where are your manners, young man? She's not here to bring you dessert. She's here to watch you till your dad gets home."

"Really?" Annie breathed, her face shining in excitement.

"Yes," Katherine replied, inexplicably thrilled by the children's acceptance.

"Wow!" David echoed. "Can you have dinner with us?"

"I think I'll be cooking dinner," Katherine replied.

"Up to you," Harmeniah commented, crimping the handles of her purse together and tugging at her cotton sweater. "Fine, then."

Once the baby-sitter was on her way, Katherine returned to the kitchen, flanked by her willing helpers. Soon she had a stir fry of chicken and vegetables started.

She glanced over at the table. "Great job. I like the pink napkins with the yellow plates."

"I picked those," Annie confided.

"I guessed you had," Katherine replied. In a moment of instant understanding, they both giggled. In typical male fashion, David rolled his eyes, but a grin lurked on his face, as well.

At that moment, Michael walked in, his gaze darting from his smiling children to a flushed Katherine. And the kitchen smelled like heaven. Certainly not like Mrs. Goode's boiled dinners. And certainly not like his own burned attempts.

But what was Katherine doing here?

She spotted him, and her face registered a variety of expressions before settling into a calm smile. "Hello, Michael."

"Katherine." He didn't keep the question from his tone.

"Harmeniah called me."

"Mrs. Goode?" He didn't know anyone had the nerve to call the woman by her first name.

Katherine smiled. "Yes. She had a personal emergency and asked if I could watch the children until you arrived home. She left you a detailed note on the hall table. It's about her sister."

"Oh." Deflated and more than a little confused, Michael nodded. Then he remembered Mrs. Goode telling him about a special doctor's appointment for her sister. Was that today?

Annie and David flung themselves at him, and he knelt down, hugging them both.

Katherine washed her hands, then turned back to him. "Well, I guess I'll be on my way."

"No!" both children protested.

"It looks like you've cooked dinner," Michael responded, still thrown by how natural she looked in his kitchen. How bewitching her flushed face appeared.

"Well, yes, but—"

"Then, won't you eat with us? Whatever it is, it smells wonderful."

She smiled again. "I think it's a little different from what the kids are used to. I hope it's okay."

"Katherine said I could eat just the chicken and rice if I don't like the vegetables," David told him.

She half shrugged an apology, but Michael couldn't

find it in himself to complain. Not when she'd rescued him from possibly losing his baby-sitter.

To his further surprise, when they began eating, David did try the vegetables. Remarkably he seemed to like them. But they were crisp, fresh and tasty. What was not to enjoy?

"This is like eating in a restaurant," Annie remarked.

Katherine smiled. "Not quite, but thanks, sweetie."

Michael bristled for a moment at the familiarity. But Annie's smile was a rainbow. One he couldn't banish with words or a look.

"That was delicious," he told Katherine honestly, as they finished. "I can't remember when I've had anything so good."

"I'm glad you enjoyed it." Katherine fiddled with the spoon in the rice bowl. "I'm sorry I didn't think about dessert."

"We could go get ice-cream cones!" David suggested gleefully.

"I want vanilla," Annie joined in. "With sprinkles."

Katherine looked at Michael helplessly.

He cleared his throat. "Hey, kids, we don't know if Katherine has other plans." David turned immediately to Katherine. "Do you?"

"Well, no, but I'm not sure your dad—"

"Daddy, can we go have ice cream? Please? Please!" It was a dual request, their voices rising in a nearly simultaneous chorus that repeated the words again and again.

It was a tide even Michael couldn't turn. "If Katherine's sure she doesn't have other plans…"

David and Annie shifted their attention to her. "You don't, do you, Katherine? Do you?"

Gracefully, she laughed. "What other plans could be better than spending the evening with you?"

It was amazing, Michael realized. Somehow, she made both of his children feel important and wanted. It was a rare gift. One his late wife had possessed, one they had fiercely missed.

As they piled into the car, twilight crept about them during their drive to the center of their old-fashioned town. Settled in the mid-1800s, primarily by German and Polish immigrants, Rosewood had been a tiny farming community until oil had been discovered. That phenomenon had propelled the village into a town, but not one so large that it encroached on the charm.

And Rosewood had retained its small town values, along with a main street that looked as though it could have been plucked from the previous century and carefully preserved.

The ice-cream parlor was housed in an ancient building, one that was painstakingly maintained. The swirls and cupolas that decorated the entrance were freshly painted. Inside, an equally well-aged, old-fashioned marble fountain dominated the space. The children clambered up on the stools at the counter.

"Do you mind?" Michael asked, wondering if she would prefer a booth.

"This is great," Katherine replied, claiming a stool for herself.

Michael took the remaining stool—the one beside her.

Pulling a menu from its holder, she glanced at him. "Don't you need to see the selections?"

He shook his head. "Nope."

She smiled. "Chocolate?"

Surprised, he angled his head toward her. "Good guess."

"Stands to reason. Anyone who would prefer straight chocolate over a s'more has to be a devotee."

Even more surprised, he studied her face. Who was this woman who noticed so much, who fit in so well, who made his children so happy?

"Sprinkles, Daddy," Annie reminded him. "Don't forget the sprinkles."

He smiled tolerantly at his youngest.

"I want strawberry *and* chocolate," David told him.

Michael caught Katherine's gaze. "And you?"

"Hmm. All the flavors look good, but I think I'll try licorice."

"Ick!" David said without hesitation.

"David!" Michael chided him.

But Katherine was laughing. "It's okay. I know I'm probably one of only a handful of people who like that flavor."

"Sort of like me not liking peanut butter?" David asked her.

"Exactly. People tease me all the time."

He nodded. "Me, too. But peanut butter tastes yucky."

"And licorice tastes yummy."

David grinned. "Uh-uh."

Michael watched their exchange. Since Ruth's death, David hadn't opened up to anyone. Yet he seemed at ease with Katherine. Katherine the preacher.

She angled her stool toward his. "I'll call the hospital when I get home, and check on Harmeniah's sister.''

Michael stopped short of thumping himself on the head. "I should have thought of that myself." Then another thought struck him. "I wonder if Mrs. Goode will be able to watch the children tomorrow."

Katherine's face was thoughtful. "If you're in a pinch, I could rearrange my morning appointments and push the afternoon ones into early evening."

"Hopefully that won't be necessary, but I appreciate the offer."

"Of course, I might demand sprinkles on *my* ice cream next time," she said with a smile.

But his expression remained sober. "I insist on paying you for your time."

She waved away his words. "Absolutely not. I enjoy the time with Annie and David. I couldn't take money for it."

"I won't ask for your help unless it's absolutely necessary."

She studied him. "I imagine it's difficult for you to take time off from work."

"I own a contracting business, and the buck stops with me. It would almost be easier if I worked for someone else. Then I could take off when necessary. But if the job doesn't get done properly on time, we stand to incur big penalties. And too many people are depending on me for their jobs. I can't forget that. When Ruth was alive, I didn't have to worry about the kids. She knew I was building a life for all of us—and a future. So when I worked late I knew they were in her hands."

Katherine hesitated. "Have you ever considered

hiring an assistant—someone who can take your place from time to time?''

He shook his head. ''It's not the same thing.''

''Agreed. But even when your wife was here to care for the children, they must have missed you when you worked such long hours.''

He studied her, wondering if there was any facet of his life she didn't feel comfortable probing into. ''I run my business and my family the way I think is best.''

''I'm not questioning that, simply voicing a thought. Like you, I prefer doing most everything myself so I'm certain it's done the way I want. In fact, it's been a liability in my work for as long as I can remember. I've had to strive to include others even when I'd feel more confident doing things myself.''

''But your work—''

''Daddy, can I have a chocolate-covered cone?'' David interrupted.

''I guess so. I don't think you'll be able to eat it all, though.''

Katherine laughed. ''But you'll have fun trying, won't you, David?''

''Yep. They make the cones here, ya know,'' David told her. ''They have this special machine, and when it's not busy the man lets you watch 'em make the cones.''

''I like to smell them baking,'' she said.

''Me, too,'' Annie chimed in. '''Specially when they make cinnamon ones.'' She looked at her father. ''Can I have a cinnamon cone, Daddy?''

He sighed. ''Why not? With all this sugar, I'll be scraping you two off the walls, anyway.''

Katherine grinned. "Me, too. One plus to the sugar, I'll get loads of stuff done tonight when I get home."

The waitress came just then and took their orders. For the next several minutes the kids popped up and down on the stools in anticipation.

Katherine gestured toward them. "It's great seeing them so happy."

Michael nodded in agreement.

"It's also great that you allowed them to come to Sunday School the past two weeks."

"Don't be too happy. It's only a temporary agreement."

She frowned. "I hope not. Annie and David need the interaction with other kids, the positive reinforcement they're receiving."

He stiffened. "I can do that for them."

"You can't do everything," she pointed out gently.

Before he could reply, the waitress brought their ice cream.

After Michael made certain the kids were settled with their cones, he dug into his own. Then he glanced over at Katherine, enjoying the look of pure satisfaction on her face. But he couldn't resist teasing her about the licorice flavor. "You realize you're eating black ice cream."

Her brows lifted as she eyed his chocolate cone. "As opposed to brown. Your point?"

"Hmm. Most women wouldn't refer to chocolate as brown."

She swallowed a lick of her ice cream. "I'm not most women."

He'd noticed, but didn't think it was wise to say so, to let her know how much she appealed to him. "So what kind of woman are you, Katherine Blake?"

She visibly swallowed, her smile leaner, more thoughtful. "I don't have a quick answer for that."

"I don't recall asking for one."

She reached for a napkin, fiddled with her cone. "Well, I'm not a small town girl...at least not originally."

Michael studied her. "Houston?"

Surprise flickered over her face. "Do you have a sideline as a psychic?"

"No. But I work with a lot of people in the oil industry. You fit the profile."

"I didn't realize I was that predictable," she countered.

"You aren't."

She turned her ice-cream cone in her fingers. "You're being very enigmatic."

"I think I'll save that label for you."

She stared at him in surprise. "Me?"

"I hadn't met you a month ago, and now my children think you hung the moon. Yet I still don't know you."

She met his eyes. "I could say the same of you, Michael."

"Daddy, Daddy," Annie called out. "Look, I got pink sprinkles, too!"

He turned to Annie, while David trotted over to Katherine's side. Their chance for a private conversation disappeared. Although Michael was pleased to see his children so happy, he found himself wanting to learn more about Katherine, about what made her tick. Yet he told himself that was a mistake...that she was already intruding too much in his thoughts.

Chapter Seven

Unable to reach Mrs. Goode at home, Katherine stopped by the hospital after she left the Carlsons. She visited with Evelyn, then offered a prayer for her as the woman was prepared for surgery, which was scheduled for the following morning.

Harmeniah followed Katherine out of the patient room into the hallway. "Thanks for seeing Evelyn, Pastor. She says she's okay, but I think she's kind of scared about tomorrow."

Katherine clasped her hand. "You'll both be in my prayers. And I'll be sure to put Evelyn's name on the church prayer roll, as well."

Harmeniah nodded but she still looked disturbed.

"Is something else bothering you?"

The older woman averted her face for a moment. "I hate to ask again, but do you think you could watch the children tomorrow? I really want to be here during Evelyn's surgery."

"Of course you do," Katherine responded. "I can

juggle my morning appointments, do a little shifting, and we're set.''

''I appreciate it, Pastor. I'll call Mr. Carlson to tell him you'll sit with the children tomorrow. I'm sure he'll be relieved.''

Katherine kept her expression benign, not certain she agreed with Harmeniah. ''Don't worry about the Carlsons, Harmeniah, and try to get a good night's sleep.''

Harmeniah's gaze strayed back to her sister's room. ''I'll try, Pastor. I guess you and I will both need some extra energy tomorrow.''

But after hours spent with the Carlson children the following day, Katherine was only reenergized. She loved their spontaneity, their fresh outlook on everything.

They were bright, energetic kids who, she was beginning to suspect, were untapped resources. At the slightest suggestion, both were creative and filled with ideas. Katherine believed they would be a joy to care for full time. But then, neither their father nor Mrs. Goode seemed able to do that.

Katherine knew there wasn't a simple solution. Michael clearly loved his children, but his job took much of his time. And it wasn't Mrs. Goode's job to be their mother.

Nor was it hers, Katherine reminded herself. Yet she couldn't repress the pleasure she felt at their least accomplishment. Together they had raked the grass beneath the huge live oak tree in the backyard, pulled weeds along the front path, then swept the area, leaving it tidy and inviting. Even Tessa had enjoyed helping before heading home.

Since the kids loved being outside, Katherine thought it would be fun to eat in the yard. Guessing that all children liked spaghetti, she'd brought over the ingredients. Luckily, she'd been given a huge basket of home-grown tomatoes by one of her church members. And she'd picked fresh basil, oregano and parsley from her own herb garden.

The kids were entranced with the fresh ingredients.

"You have your own garden?" David asked, smelling the soft, fragrant basil.

"Well, it's kind of small, but I love fresh ingredients."

"Could we plant a garden?" Annie asked.

"Well...I think you'll have to ask your dad about that."

"Will you help us make one?" David asked.

She hesitated. Michael Carlson might not be pleased with any long-term plans. "Why don't we talk to your dad first, make sure that he wants a garden."

"Okay," David agreed. "Are you going to be here tomorrow?"

Katherine had made a discreet call to the hospital and learned that Harmeniah's sister had come through surgery all right. She hadn't talked to the sitter, though, and didn't yet know her plans for the following day.

"Perhaps when your dad comes home he can talk to Mrs. Goode, and we'll know."

When everything was ready, they assembled at the table in the yard. The gate creaked as it opened, and the kids jumped to their feet.

"Daddy!"

Annie and David ran toward their father, landing

against him with twin thuds. His muscled body didn't flinch. Instead, he scooped them both up, and for a few moments all three voices sounded at once. As Katherine watched them she couldn't completely sort the feelings their tableau evoked...pleasure...warmth... envy.

Before she could wonder further, they converged around the table. In the babble, she greeted Michael, saw the appreciation in his eyes.

"This looks great, Katherine. I'll wash up and be right back."

"Hurry, Daddy!" the children urged.

True to his word, Michael returned quickly, taking the seat across from her, just as though this were their little family. Immediately, a seed of fear sprouted.

Fear that said this all seemed too comfortable, too much like what she'd been dreaming of. And she knew this picture wasn't in her future. No man deserved the kind of wife she was fated to be. Especially not this man who had two such very special children.

More quiet than usual, she allowed the children to chat with their father. They bubbled over, relaying what they'd done that day. He promised to look at their accomplishments as soon as they had eaten.

"I don't want to let dinner get cold," he told them. Then he caught Katherine's attention. "You shouldn't have gone to so much trouble. We're not used to gourmet food."

"Good," she replied. "This is just spaghetti."

"Considering the spaghetti I cook comes in cans, this is gourmet to us."

"It's the fresh tomatoes. It's hard to make anything taste bad when you have home-grown tomatoes in the mix."

Despite her light tone, he said seriously, "Thank you, Katherine. Mrs. Goode's absence could have been really traumatic for the kids. Nothing has been very stable for them since their mother's death. So I appreciate today."

Emotions still stirred, she took a deep breath, repressing any qualms or regrets at what she was about to say. "It sounds like you need a friend, Michael. I could be one…a friend, that is."

A beat of unexpected silence thrummed between them. One that said the tension between them signaled far more than mere friendship.

Finally he nodded. "I suppose I could use a friend."

She ignored a sharp jab of misgiving that proclaimed she wanted to be more than friends, that her words had been a mistake. "Then, it's a deal."

"Daddy." David snagged his father's attention. "Can we make a garden?"

Michael dragged his gaze away from Katherine. "What?"

"A garden, Daddy."

"So we can have fresh stuff," Annie added. "Please?"

"I don't see anything wrong with a garden, but it's an awful lot of work. Where'd you get this idea?"

"Katherine has a garden," David explained.

"She pulls fresh burbs out of it," Annie explained.

"Herbs," Katherine clarified. "I put some in the sauce."

Michael had an odd look on his face, one she couldn't interpret. Then he shrugged. "My grandparents always had a garden, and I don't think it hurt me to work in it."

"Is that yes?" David asked.

"Sure."

Satisfied, the kids turned their attention back to the spaghetti. Katherine, her appetite diminished now that Michael had accepted her offer of friendship, looked toward the house, gently outlined by the fading light. It was the kind of house that seemed to promise happy families...a couple still in love with each other after fifty years of marriage. The kind of happily-ever-after that wasn't in her future.

"I really like your home... It has that 'step inside and stay a while' quality." Immediately embarrassed, she realized the words must have sounded as though she wanted yet another invitation.

But he spoke before she could correct the impression. "You know it's always seemed that way to me, too, real comforting. But Ruth always wanted a new house...in one of those subdivisions they're building outside town."

Katherine thought those houses all looked the same, without the distinction or charm of Michael's home. But most of her contemporaries loved them. They found the new homes modern and sleek. And she'd noticed most were filled with young, happy-looking families. Perhaps she was the one out of step, Katherine realized.

"I planned to get one for her," Michael continued, his voice growing flat. "But I waited too long. Funny. I always thought we had forever. I never guessed we didn't even have tomorrow."

For a brief, insane moment Katherine envied Ruth Carlson, the love she had shared with Michael, their idyllic children. As instantly she was ashamed.

"I suspect she knew your intentions," Katherine

murmured. "And sometimes that's almost as good as the reality."

Michael shrugged, an unhappy movement that signaled his pain. "I don't know. I thought she would be cured, as well." Then his expression grew challenging. "At least, that's what I prayed for."

Katherine bent her head for a moment, remembering her own past, the pain of her parents' broken marriage, their fractured family. "Not all prayer is answered in ways we expect."

"It's not answered period." Bitterness flavored the words.

"If you pray for rain and get a monsoon, is that an answer, a solution or a surprise?"

"It's a disaster," he replied flatly.

"Daddy, what are we going to plant?" Annie asked, startling them both.

He took a deep breath. "What do you want to plant, princess?"

She smiled. "What you like, Daddy."

How could he not believe, Katherine wondered, with two such perfect and wonderful children? They alone were proof of everything good.

"Daddy likes those green things," David supplied.

Katherine's and Michael's eyes met, unexpected amusement flowing between them.

Michael cleared his throat. "Any particular green, son?"

"Like on the pizza," David explained.

"You're right!" Michael glanced at Katherine. "I like all kinds of peppers."

"Then we'll plant peppers," Annie told him.

"And sometimes it's nice to put a few flowers in

the vegetable garden,'' Katherine commented. ''It adds beauty to the practicality.''

Again an unfathomable expression crossed Michael's face.

''I like pink flowers,'' Annie told her.

''Me, too,'' Katherine agreed. ''Especially roses.''

''Not me,'' David objected.

''I don't know, son. There are few things in this world as incredible as a perfect rose or a beautiful woman, and usually, you'll find the two together.''

Something warm curled in Katherine's stomach. She knew Michael Carlson was a special man, but she hadn't expected a soul filled with romance, or for him to possess the words of a poet.

''Okay,'' David answered with a shrug. ''Guess they won't hurt the other stuff.''

''Spoken like a diplomat, son.''

Katherine looked between father and son. It was more than diplomacy. It was the kind of special relationship this family shared. One she'd always wanted to be part of. One she'd never had, one she could never hope for. Once again Katherine was standing on the outside looking in.

Michael rushed home. Although Katherine had agreed to watch the children, he had insisted it wouldn't be more than a day or so. Now, a week-and-a-half later, she was still helping him. Mrs. Goode's sister was doing well, but she needed care during her recuperation.

Michael didn't know what he would have done without Katherine's help. She was truly becoming a good friend.

And maybe that's what was sticking in his craw.

The fact that she wanted them to be friends, nothing else. Even though he told himself he didn't want anything to do with a minister, he was still immensely attracted to Katherine. There was something about her spontaneity, her fresh approach to life that was incredibly appealing.

He should be grateful, he supposed, that she only wanted friendship, since he had no intention of returning to the church.

But he couldn't repress an image of her face…the laughter that lurked in her eyes…or her lips parted as she enjoyed a simple ice-cream cone. Katherine's enthusiasm had been as refreshing as a child's; her appeal, however, was completely womanly.

Reaching his house, Michael headed not inside but to the gate that opened to the backyard. He knew where Katherine and his children would be.

Under Katherine's direction, the kids had staked out a garden, tilled the soil and worked like little Trojans to plant a variety of vegetables and flowers. At her suggestion, they had each planted a rosebush in honor of their mother. The gesture had touched him deeply.

Stepping farther into the yard, he saw that Katherine and the kids were all on their hands and knees in the dirt, digging new rows. Yet Michael could see that, in typical fashion, Katherine had managed to infuse the project with fun. They were all laughing over some shared joke.

Katherine spotted him first. Her face changed like the shading of a windswept day. Initially it shone in welcome, then the storm clouds moved in. And he wondered why. Was there something hidden beneath her seeming openness?

Then Annie and David saw him and ran to greet him. He took dirt clumps and kisses with equal aplomb.

"Daddy!" Annie exclaimed. "We're planting corn!"

"Oh?"

"Uh-huh. 'Cause David likes it."

"That's a good reason, princess."

David shuffled, looking pleased but embarrassed. "Not just for me."

"Agreed," Michael told him. "We all like it."

Katherine stood up, dusting the dirt from her bare knees. The late-afternoon sun glinted off her long dark hair, which she had pulled into an impish ponytail. Wearing a sleeveless top and shorts, she could have passed for a teenager.

"Are you about through with the garden for today?" Michael asked.

"Yes. I think we're all ready to get cleaned up."

"Then, why don't we go for dinner?" Michael suggested.

Katherine glanced down at her casual outfit.

"To Casa Boñita in old town," he continued. It was a decidedly casual restaurant that served the best Mexican food for miles.

She nodded. "Sounds great."

Just then, the French doors on the patio opened, and Mrs. Goode stepped out. The kids ran to greet her, and the older woman looked pleased by the welcome. However, once the hellos were aside they showered her with details about the garden Katherine was helping them plant.

Katherine, however, kept the woman from thinking she'd been so easily supplanted. "Your shoes are difficult to fill, Harmeniah. I know the kids are thrilled to see you.''

"Well, Pastor, I know they've been in good hands.''

"They miss you,'' Katherine replied graciously.

"Will you be back with us soon?'' Michael asked, knowing he couldn't have Katherine caring for his children…for so many reasons.

"I still need to help my sister, but she's on the mend, so I can come back part-time. Of course, if you want to look for another sitter, I'll understand.''

As though there were any available. Michael shook his head. "We'll work around it, Mrs. Goode.''

She visited with the children a bit more before leaving. Then Michael sent David and Annie inside to wash faces and hands, turning at last to Katherine.

"I appreciate your help, but I don't expect you to continue caring for the kids. It should be easier to find a part-time sitter than a full-time one.''

"I'll do whatever I can while you're in a pinch. Luckily summer tends to be slower at church, so I have more time.''

"I'm not sure that's a good idea.'' He knew he sounded reluctant.

For a moment something akin to disappointment blossomed in Katherine's expression, before she composed her features. Still her eyes knowing, her voice strained, she asked, "Because I'm a minister?''

"I've been telling you how much I don't want my children involved in church. And you represent everything I'm opposed to. You're a minister, Katherine, and nothing will change that.''

A flicker of pain appeared in her eyes, then was gone. "Which is why I can be a good friend to you.

I don't judge, Michael. That's neither my job nor my way of doing things."

"We're at opposite ends of the planet in this matter, Katherine. And I don't believe for a moment that you can't see that, as well."

"I agree that we disagree. But that doesn't mean I can't care about your family."

"And convince my children that I'm wrong, that they shouldn't listen to me?"

Hurt filled her eyes, and for a moment her lips trembled. "Do you really think I would do that? Try to turn children away from their father?"

He passed a hand over his forehead. "I don't know. I guess not. But you have to admit that they can't wait to attend whatever's going on at church."

"That's because they enjoy what's taught there, the interaction with other kids," she pointed out gently. "And since you took them to church before their mother passed away, it comes naturally to them. Children learn by example, not by words. Until the past year, going to church *was* their example."

Logically Michael knew she was right. Yet he was unable to repress the feeling that she couldn't be simply a friend—not when she was a minister. He refused to examine whether there was more to his agitation—that her easy decision to be only friends had been galling him.

Still, the words didn't come easily. "I really do appreciate what you've done for the kids...and me."

Something unfathomable flashed in her eyes. If he didn't know better he would think it was regret.

"That's what friends are for."

Chapter Eight

Katherine took her battered psyche along with her as she continued to help Michael care for his children in Mrs. Goode's absence. The older woman had opted for mornings, and Katherine took over after lunch until their father arrived home.

Michael hadn't been able to find another sitter, even part-time. He couldn't be absent from his current contracting project, and he didn't want to put the kids in day care.

Knowing that, Katherine couldn't allow their strained feelings to affect the children. Innocent, all accepting, they continued to be a joy.

She reminded herself of that when the hurt surfaced. It had been a shock to learn that Michael felt so strongly about her job. She had begun to believe that he had been able to view her differently—as a person...a woman, not a minister.

But maybe that wasn't possible. Not even with a man like Michael. He resented everything she was, everything she represented. There wasn't even a question of his viewing her only as a woman. That debate was over.

Annie and David were a balm to that heartache. Annie, sensing she was down, had drawn her a beautiful red heart. Even David had helped, giving her one of his prized toy soldiers for her own. Realizing how lucky she was to have them even on a temporary basis, she pulled herself out of her funk, vowing to enjoy every moment.

Which was why she had dug out the bicycles in the garage, filling the low tires and making sure they were roadworthy. Together, the three of them rode to the park. They played on the swings, slides and jungle gym. Each moment reinforced what Katherine had guessed all along. Nothing was quite as fulfilling as kids, a family.

Even though she had to shuffle appointments and commitments, Katherine wouldn't have traded a moment of this precious time. Cindy had volunteered to help with sick calls, and she'd also taken on much of Katherine's paperwork and correspondence.

Luckily, her friend was a trust fund baby, thanks to the oil business. Although Cindy volunteered for nearly a dozen organizations and sat on the board of her family's oil company, most of her time was free, allowing her to help Katherine.

"Katherine, do we really hafta go home?" David asked as they pedaled away from the park, interrupting Katherine's thoughts.

"Yes. Your dad may be home soon. You don't want him worrying, do you?"

"No," Annie replied for them both. "Daddy worries lots already."

The comment surprised Katherine. Not because she

didn't think the children were perceptive, but because she didn't picture Michael worrying so that it showed.

"Maybe we could bring Daddy back here," David offered, always the negotiator.

"Tell you what. If we get home in time to make a picnic supper, we can ask him. But that's only if he's home early enough, okay?"

"Sometimes he has to work *real* late," Annie told her with a small sigh.

"I know, sweetie. But that's so he can provide a nice home and a good future for you and David. I'm sure he'd rather be at the park with you having a picnic."

David grinned. "Or playing softball."

Katherine glanced at him. "Does he like softball?"

"He was the best player on the team," David replied with pride.

"Doesn't he still play?"

Annie shook her head. "Not since Mommy died."

Apparently Michael had given up everything when he'd lost his wife, even the sport of softball. Although she was deeply touched, Katherine made her voice purposely cheerful. "If we hurry home, we'll probably have time to make that picnic supper."

"I can go kinda fast," Annie offered.

"Not too fast," Katherine cautioned. "We won't save time if we fall and scrape our knees." And the mid-July day was hot.

David grinned. "I can go fast without falling."

Katherine glanced over at Annie. "Well, I'm afraid I can't, so you'll have to hold back a little for me."

Even allowing for the youngest member of their trio, they made good time. Annie and David raced to the front door, burst into the kitchen.

Katherine brought up the rear, teasing them. "First one in the kitchen gets to clean up."

Twin squeaks from their tennis shoes skidding to a halt made her grin. She pushed open the swinging door, walking to stand beside them. "Looks like a three-way tie."

Annie and David both giggled, and soon they were collecting the ingredients for a simple lunch.

"What about Daddy's bike?" David asked.

"Good point. Why don't we check the tires? But in case your Dad's tired, let's give him the option of going by bike or car. *If* he agrees to go," she stressed.

"Okay," David conceded.

Since it looked as though the kids might burst if they waited for their father to come home, Katherine suggested they go into the backyard and jump on the trampoline for a while. But once outside, the kids insisted that she join them. It didn't take much coaxing. Katherine loved bouncing with them, making them shriek. And her attention was focused fully on them, when Michael stepped out the French doors of the patio.

He paused, watching his children frolic with Katherine. It struck Michael again—his disbelief that she could be a minister. It seemed she ought to enjoy more pastoral pursuits, certainly more calm, dignified ones.

But there was nothing dignified about her at the moment. Bouncing alongside his children, her hair was flung out like a dark, silk banner. And her long, tanned legs pumped in unison with David's and Annie's.

Maybe it was a good thing she *was* a minister. It made her far easier to resist, he told himself.

But his resistance was wavering. He wanted nothing more than to take her in his arms, to test his suspicion that she would fit perfectly there.

The children spotted him, waving as they bounced. He walked to the edge of the trampoline. "Looks like everyone's having fun."

Katherine slowed her jumping, her face flushing slightly. "Hi."

"Hey," he replied.

The children scrambled toward him, talking excitedly about the picnic in the park at the same time.

When they'd finished, he studied Katherine's expression.

Her lips edged upward, not her usual grin but a more restrained smile. "We made a simple supper and packed it in the picnic basket, because the kids had such a good time at the park this afternoon."

"Dare I ask what having air in the tires means?"

"We rode bikes to the park, but I reminded Annie and David that you might be tired after working all day and not feel like biking to the park. That is, *if* you feel like having supper at the park."

He was exhausted but he didn't want his kids to know that. Even more, he didn't want them to think his time spent with them was unimportant. "Sounds great. You sure the bikes are really in shape?"

"Katherine knows how to fix 'em," David informed him.

"By necessity," she explained. "As a kid I had to keep my own maintained. And since I still love biking, I kept up the skill."

"Great."

They carried the basket and thermos to the bikes and divided the load between the adult cycles. Briefly

Michael remembered the last time the bikes had been taken out. It had been before Ruth had gotten sick…and they'd been abandoned ever since.

Even though the bikes were a painful reminder, he knew he couldn't ignore every activity he'd shared with his late wife. Seeing how excited the children were, Michael was immediately remorseful that he'd put away everything associated with Ruth at their expense.

And David was right—Katherine had checked out the bike, filled the tires, and it was in perfect shape. Only the memories assailing him seemed off kilter.

Then his eyes landed on Annie and David, excitedly pedaling ahead. As Katherine had said, maybe it was time to fold away some of the remembrances, because even though it seemed obscenely unfair, life *did* go on.

Katherine pulled up at his side, her voice quiet. "It occurred to me that it might be difficult for you watching me ride Ruth's bike. I'm happy to put it back in the garage. You don't need me along on this picnic. The kids will understand."

"But I won't," he responded, surprising them both. "You once asked if I trotted out morbid memories for the kids. I didn't think so, but I've attached a kind of hands-off mentality to anything associated with Ruth. And that's not fair to them…or to her, either. She wouldn't have wanted that."

"I didn't know her, but I suspect you're right. I can see a lot of her in your children. They wouldn't be so open and generous without special guidance from an exceptional person."

Michael's throat thickened. How was it that Katherine knew the right thing to say…in fact, seemed to know how he was feeling? Others had tried to talk to him about Ruth but it had been incredibly difficult for him. Each person who'd asked him to open up had simply made him close that much more. It was as though Katherine invited Ruth in, as though there was room for the three of them in their conversation.

Some of his exhaustion fell away with the realization. Together they pedaled toward the park. A light breeze rippled through the evening air, teasing them with the promise of a cooler evening ahead.

Seeing that Michael was staring ahead, Katherine angled her head to study his profile. What was he thinking about? she wondered. Was he immersed in memories of his late wife, or was it possible he had moved past them just a bit?

It was difficult to know. Michael wasn't an open person. She didn't know if he'd been that way always, or just since his wife's death. Katherine also didn't know if she was aggravating the situation by being part of the church he resented so deeply.

Within a short time, they arrived at the park. David and Annie picked a table close to the playground equipment.

"Can we swing, Daddy?" Annie pleaded.

"Please?" David added.

Michael glanced at Katherine. "Can the supper you packed wait a while?"

"Sure."

"Okay," he told them.

They flung their bikes to the ground and scampered toward the swings and slides.

"Think they'll miss us?" Michael asked wryly, leaning his own bike against a nearby tree.

She managed a partial grin as she dismounted. "Probably when they get hungry."

"That's better," he responded.

Katherine looked at him in question.

"The smile. I was wondering where it had disappeared to."

Uncomfortable, she shrugged, parking her bike next to his. "I'm not sure what you mean."

"I think you do."

Since she did, Katherine couldn't argue the point. Instead, she opened the picnic basket, pulled out a tablecloth.

He took one end, and together they draped the multicolored fabric over the redwood table. As she smoothed the tablecloth in place, Michael retrieved the thermos.

In tacit agreement, Katherine pulled the cups from the basket and he filled them.

"Did you want to swing with the kids?" Michael asked.

She shook her head. "I think I did enough of that earlier today. But you go ahead."

"I'd rather just sit here and talk for a while, if you don't mind."

That elusive feeling of warmth began to curl inside her. "I'd like that, actually."

And for a while they discussed the mundane, the specifics of the day...the light and easy. Which made Katherine that much more unprepared for his next words.

"You've never told me—how did you come to be a minister?"

For a moment she caught her breath. Again the past

swirled over her...and between them. "I'm not sure there's one easy answer."

"Then start with part one," he suggested.

"Part one," she mused. For a moment her eyes closed briefly, a defense against memories and also a silent request for strength. "Well, to begin with, I come from a long line of ministers."

"Really?" He looked only slightly surprised. "Your father?"

"Actually," she paused. "My mother."

His eyebrows shot up in shock. "Your *mother?*"

"She was a pioneer in the field. She certainly wasn't the first female minister, but it was a select group. And she was a natural for the job. She possessed a mountain of energy, always taking on more and more projects and stray people. Then and now, she's the strongest woman I've ever known. Her example both inspired and challenged."

"And you wanted to be like her?"

Irony flashed through Katherine's thoughts, but she schooled the impulse to tell him the entire truth. "Actually, I admired that she cared more about her calling than any obstacles she encountered. And she made me care about others more than myself. When most kids were hanging out at the mall, I was volunteering at the soup kitchen. It's something I've never forgotten."

"So you followed in her footsteps."

Katherine flinched inwardly. "In some ways."

"Is that where you learned to balance everything in your life?"

History told her that balance didn't exist for women in strong roles such as her own. "You forget, I don't have a family to add to the equation."

His voice was even. "No, I didn't forget."

She wondered painfully if she'd sprouted the equivalent of a sign across her forehead announcing herself as hopelessly, terminally single. But she pushed away the thought. "I do worry when my job gets between me and friends."

"Is that a not-too-subtle hint?"

"Sort of. My calling should make it easier for me to relate to my friends, rather than be an obstacle."

"It won't be...as long as you don't try to preach to me," he warned.

"Have I done that?" Katherine asked softly, wishing just for the moment that so much baggage didn't exist between them.

"I suppose not," he replied truthfully. "But I expect it to happen."

"That's difficult to fight—expectation."

"Yes..." He hesitated. "I'm very aware of that."

Their eyes met across the table. An unexpected hunger surfaced, crying out to be recognized. In the quiet, repressed need thrummed between them. The need of two wounded people who were afraid to trust, to believe.

And somewhere in the exchange, she felt another nudge of awareness, one that only increased as he sat next to her on the bench.

The ripe smell of full flowering honeysuckle drifted toward them in the lazy evening breeze. It was a hushed twilight disturbed by only the occasional cry of the children at play.

The moment was one she wanted to preserve in time, then keep close on lonely nights. Lonely nights that seemed to stretch out forever in her future.

Michael met her eyes just then, and Katherine wished desperately that that didn't have to be so. That he could share her future and warm all those coming nights.

Chapter Nine

Michael entered his house at the end of the following week, mulling over something that had been bothering him for days. Despite his theological differences with Katherine, he was extremely grateful for her help. Over the past weeks, she had been invaluable in caring for the children.

Not only that, but she had held his family together, suggesting outings, simple dinners, times when they could be together. Times for healing. It was a lot to be grateful for.

Especially since he'd had to work extremely late several evenings—like tonight. And yet he'd done nothing to thank her—to show her the extent of his gratitude. His search for another baby-sitter had been fruitless. His only alternative would be to place them in day care, and Katherine had been adamant about helping rather then place them outside of the home since they were still adjusting to the loss of their mother.

Walking into the kitchen, Michael could smell the

remains of dinner. And the house was quiet. Katherine wasn't in sight.

She must be upstairs, Michael decided as he headed that direction, guessing he would find his children in their rooms. It was a good guess. David was tucked into bed, his hands flung upward on the pillow, his breathing deep. Michael smoothed the blanket, gently kissed David's forehead, and then crept from the room.

Heading down the hall, he was entering Annie's room, when the sound of soft singing halted his steps.

Craning his head, he could view the room more easily. One night-light remained on, illuminating the occupants. Katherine sat beside Annie's bed in the wicker rocker that had once been Ruth's. As his wife had often done, Katherine was singing to young Annie. But there the resemblance ended.

While Ruth's voice had been sweet and melodious, Katherine's was richer—a husky sound that captured him. Standing in the dark hallway, he was supremely aware of her as a woman. Not a minister, not a friend, simply a woman.

Terrified by how drawn he was to her, Michael turned around, exiting the hallway before Katherine could discover him. Downstairs, he occupied his hands by making a fresh pot of coffee. Despite the late hour, he felt the need for a cup of warm, bracing brew.

Scarcely a few minutes later, he heard the light tread of Katherine's footsteps on the stairs.

Spotting him, her face first registered surprise, then pleasure. "You're home."

"At long last. I'm sorry I'm so late. Coffee?"

She shook her head. "Not for me. It would keep me up all night."

He clasped his own mug more firmly, unwilling to let her know that his own sleep would be disturbed, as well. By thoughts of her. He cleared his suddenly constricted throat. "Did you and the children have a good day?"

She smiled, remembering. "It was especially good. The kids are thrilled because the plants in their garden are growing like wildfire. Annie's already planning the meal she wants to cook for you with the crop."

"So it's a *crop* now?"

Katherine grinned. "Absolutely. If we manage even one full-grown pepper and tomato, it will be a smashing success."

"Somehow, I suspect you will."

Then the uneasiness he was feeling spilled out between them, making the silence awkward.

Michael swallowed a sip of coffee. "I've been thinking about something..."

When he hesitated, she filled the gap. "Yes?"

"Actually it's about how much you're doing for Annie and David, for all of us. I honestly don't know how I would have managed without your help."

"I told you I was happy to do it."

"It's more than that," Michael managed to say. "You've been good for them." He stopped short of including himself in the statement. "And I'd like to try to repay you."

"I told you I wouldn't take money—"

"Several times," he replied wryly. "But I want to do *something*. Does your house need anything fixed, maybe some custom shelving, a remodeled bathroom?"

She shook her head. "No, my place is in pretty good shape, but I could use your offer somewhere else."

He met her eyes warily, an uncanny suspicion assailing him. "You don't mean—"

"The church building is old, and there are several things that need fixing, things we can't afford to have done. You already noticed our ancient wiring system."

Michael groaned. "The *church* building?" It was a modest request, but one he didn't think he could grant.

"You did ask," she reminded him. "Of course, you're under no obligation to help. I've told you I'm happy to care for the children."

Michael turned for a moment, staring out the window into the darkness. Everything inside him balked.

Katherine's voice softened. "It's not emotional blackmail, Michael. Forget I said anything."

For a long time only quiet lay between them.

Michael considered his choices, realizing he had only one. "I don't suppose I have to believe in a client's business to work for them. That can apply to the church, as well."

"I'm beginning to feel bad, Michael. Please forget I said anything."

He sighed. "I'm not built that way, Katherine. I can't simply take without giving back."

"It is a human failing," she agreed. "One most of us share."

He'd made up his mind. "Since tomorrow's Saturday, why don't I plan to meet you there in the morning. I can look over what needs repair and get started."

"Only if you insist," she replied.

However, there was a mischievous glint in her eye. He had a sneaking suspicion he'd just been neatly maneuvered. Yet it *had* been his idea. Hadn't it?

Michael hadn't known it would affect him so to enter the church sanctuary, which he had studiously avoided on previous visits.

It was a race between the clutching of his stomach and the pain in his heart to determine just how he felt. And somewhere in between he stood, flanked by bitterness and sadness.

The hushed quiet was accentuated by the soaring ceiling that swept majestically over the building. Ancient beams anchored the structure. And simple but graceful stained-glass windows filtered the light that dappled over equally old pews.

Michael's throat tightened as he fought the feelings that simply stepping in the building evoked. He had been raised to attend church as naturally as he sat down to dinner each evening. And it was difficult to suppress the memories and emotions that went with that upbringing. Despite his resistance, they were swamping him.

He could easily envision his close friends who had been raised as he had, the activities they had shared. His youth group had been his core of friends, the nucleus of his social life. They were the kind of friends he could still call on today with any problem and know they could be depended upon. They were also friends who wouldn't understand his segregation from the church and who would also, with only good intentions, try to drag him back into the fold.

And if his parents had still been alive they would

have been deeply disappointed to learn he'd turned away from the church. In some ways Michael was glad he had moved from his hometown to Rosewood. If he were still there, he would have felt his separation from the church even more keenly.

Michael gazed upward again, imagining all the prayers sent heavenward in this house. Bitterly he wondered how many like his own had gone unanswered. This hadn't been his church, but that didn't change his feelings. God hadn't answered his prayers, or those of his friends and family who had also prayed for Ruth. That door had been relentlessly slammed shut.

Katherine's voice as she spoke was soft, yet it still startled him. "I'm sorry to have kept you waiting."

He suspected the delay on her part had been deliberate, either to give him more time to collect himself, or to encourage him to ponder his faith. He didn't especially want to decide which at the moment.

"No problem."

"As you know, it's a very old building."

"I'd guess mid-to late-nineteenth century."

She smiled. "You guess right. The original stone structure was built in 1853. It's been added on to over the years."

"It's an impressive building."

"I think it was important to the immigrants who settled here to have something so permanent and solid. They were a long way from home." She paused. "I'm sorry. I sound like a tour guide, but this church's history has always fascinated me."

He nodded. "It's okay. Knowing the age of the building can help in making some repairs."

"Why don't I show you around." She led him on

a tour of the building, pointing out some cracked plaster, several leaks that had stained the ceiling, and a few other minor repairs. "I hope the roof is stable," she told him. "We really can't afford the cost of a new one."

"I'll go up top, see what kind of shape it's in."

"Great. Oh, and there's one more thing. The lights in the hallway and my office flicker quite a bit."

He remembered the frayed cords he'd seen. "I'll check it out."

She smiled. "I really appreciate this. Although the building is impressive, our budget isn't."

"It's little enough to repay what you've done for my family."

"I'm happy to do it—really. Annie and David add a dimension to my life..." She paused. "A very special dimension."

"I'm glad you think you've gained something from the situation, too, and that it's not all one-sided."

Her voice deepened, a husky contralto. "You needn't worry about that."

Studying her, he wondered if he imagined the faint coloring in her cheeks, the brightening of her eyes. Then she busied herself with the papers in her hands, and he guessed he must have imagined the changes.

"I'll go up on the roof first," he told her.

"Whatever you think best. You're the expert."

He hesitated.

She met his gaze. "Is there something else?"

"Yes. Would you like to go to dinner tonight?"

She froze for a moment. "Dinner?"

"Doing the repairs is one way of saying thank-you, but you've been feeding my kids for weeks. Wouldn't you like a dinner cooked by someone else? Mrs. Goode has agreed to watch David and Annie.''

Katherine met his gaze, hers again seeming to brighten. ''That would be lovely.''

''Eight o'clock all right?''

She nodded. ''I'll look forward to it. Um...I live in the rectory two houses east of the church.'' Katherine fiddled with the papers in her hands once more, but she didn't look at them. ''I suppose I should leave you to the repairs.''

He watched as she disappeared in the direction of her office. The dinner invitation had been an impulse. He just hoped it wasn't a mistake, that she wouldn't realize how affected by her he really was.

Then it occurred to him that she probably wouldn't treat it like a real date. He sighed, wondering why his relief was turning to disappointment.

''What do you think?'' Katherine asked as she pulled out yet another dress from her closet, holding it up for her friend's inspection.

''Fine, if you're going to a funeral,'' Cindy told her frankly.

''What's wrong with it?''

''Where should I begin?'' Cindy retorted.

''That bad?''

''Absolutely. I know you own pretty clothes. Is there some hidden motive for dressing ugly tonight?''

Katherine held the dress up to her chest and peered into the mirror. ''I want to make the right kind of impression.''

''That you're matronly and dull?''

Letting the dress slide down, Katherine turned to

her friend. "Actually, I want to look like the kind of person who could have a husband and children."

Cindy grabbed her hands. "Oh, Katiecakes! You *are* the kind of person who can have the perfect family. But don't you see...you can't pretend to be someone you're not." For a moment the pain of Cindy's own past surfaced in her eyes. "Trust me. That doesn't work. You're not a reserved, stuffed potato. You're you. And that's great. You have style, color, warmth, panache!"

"Panache?" Katherine repeated skeptically.

"You betcha. Don't you see how special you are? I know men might be a little intimidated by the minister thing, but Michael's past that. He's seen how wonderful you are. His late wife may have been the traditional type." Cindy's voice softened; she was awash in her own memories. "That doesn't mean you should try to change who you are."

Katherine looked down at the decidedly drab dress. "I suppose you're right. If I remember correctly, I bought this for a job interview when I was in college." Her voice grew small. "Somehow I thought it might be more suitable for tonight."

Cindy's voice gentled even more, her words guided by the heartbreak of her own experience. "If Michael doesn't like you for who you are, he's not the one for you."

Katherine lifted her eyes. "But I sure hope he is."

"The one?" Cindy asked softly.

"And only." Even as she voiced the words, Katherine felt her heart clutch, remembering her past...and her legacy.

Cindy tried to lighten her mood. "Don't look so

worried. Love's supposed to be about happiness, re-member?''

If only that were so, Katherine thought in despair. If only.

Michael fiddled with his blazer. Although it was freshly pressed from the cleaners, he wasn't certain about his choice. Maybe he should have worn a suit.

Deciding that he was being ridiculous, Michael rang the doorbell. After all, it wasn't a date. Just a thank-you dinner.

Katherine opened the door and those illusions fell away. From head to toe, she was a bright splash of color. Her dazzling red dress was the perfect foil for her long, dark hair, which fell in gentle waves. The overwhelming impression was one of complete fem-ininity, from the earrings that teased with subtle spar-kle to her strappy high heels. She looked at once el-egant and enticing.

Swallowing, Michael wondered how he had sent such a misguided message. Or had he? The way she looked, he couldn't possibly consider this any less than a full-fledged date. And maybe that's what he'd wanted all along, what he'd denied to himself.

''Michael.'' She greeted him. ''Won't you come in?''

Gingerly he stepped inside, surprise slowing his pace. He wasn't certain what he'd expected. He'd thought she would live in a rather drab house deco-rated primarily with religious art. Which made Kath-erine's house that much more of a shock.

The walls were painted deep peach, a warmly in-viting, almost terra-cotta color. And those walls were covered with beautiful works of art, some traditional, some wildly modern. Her furniture was much the same. Antiques coexisted alongside a sleekly contemporary sofa. The room was oddly both invigorating and soothing. Much like Katherine herself.

As he absorbed the surroundings, a small white dog flew toward him.

"And this is Snowy," Katherine told him, "my not terribly ferocious companion."

Michael knelt down to pet the West Highland terrier, who responded by licking his hand. "He's a friendly little guy."

"For the most part. But only if he likes you. He's never mean, but he can be standoffish. You seem to have won him over."

"I like animals, always have."

Katherine cocked her head. "But you don't have any pets."

"I was waiting until Annie was old enough. Then...."

"Of course," she murmured. Then she bent to pet Snowy. "If you don't mind them being around dogs, I could bring Snowy by, see how the kids interact with him."

"Good idea." Michael's gaze traveled over her again, his voice deepening. "You seem to have a lot of them."

Her gaze snapped upward, meeting his. As suddenly, he was certain she realized they weren't talking only about the dog.

But no words passed between them, only an awareness that grew in the silence...that fermented in the glance they shared.

"I made a reservation at the Heidelberg," he finally managed to say, dragging his attention away. "I hope that's okay."

She picked up her purse from a slender hall table, toying with the clasp, her voice overly bright. "Sounds wonderful. It's my favorite."

Once inside Michael's SUV, the dim interior seemed very intimate. Previous times in the vehicle had always included the kids. Now the surroundings seemed very adult, very different. It was a short ride to the restaurant, but the awareness in the car was at a pinnacle.

The Heidelberg had originally been a two-story stone house built by one of Rosewood's more prominent pioneers. It had been converted in the fifties to a restaurant and was considered the nicest one in their small town. The family who operated the business had invested well in period pieces. Some were decorative, but the bulk of their collection consisted of antique tables and chairs. Massive, rustic nineteenth-century chandeliers hung throughout the main dining room and candles lit the individual tables. Ivy wound up the stone walls, spilling over the arched doorways, while fresh flowers filled crystal vases.

Glancing at Katherine as they waited to be seated, Michael realized she fit in perfectly here. As perfectly as she fit in at backyard barbecues and suppers in the park. It was a rare woman who could.

She met his gaze, her lips tipping upward. "Can you imagine how the original owners would feel knowing their mini mansion was turned into something so *commercial?*"

His own lips twitched. "Mini mansion?"

"Don't you envision them as rather proper, even stuffy, upper-crust pillars of the community? Of course, at that time the entire community probably consisted of half a dozen buildings and maybe one street. Not much to be a pillar of.''

His grin turned into a chuckle. ''Isn't that a bit irreverent?''

She grinned, looking pleased. ''You think so?''

Before he could reply, the hostess approached, then led them to a table across from the huge fireplace. Since it was July, only a small fire had been laid. Still, the flames of the fire echoed those of the candles.

Katherine's face looked incredibly soft in the low light. It wasn't an impression he'd noticed before. She always seemed so strong, so in charge. Now she appeared utterly feminine.

Michael didn't even notice the food as the courses came and went. Instead, the conversation consumed him. Conversation uninterrupted by children. It dawned on him that he hadn't enjoyed an evening so much since…well, in over a year-and-a-half.

Like a breath of fresh air, Katherine continued to surprise him. And in these surroundings he could almost forget that she was a minister.

Almost.

As they ate, an ensemble music group started playing. The music sounded more American than German, but the diners didn't seem to mind, many taking to the generous dance area.

Michael met Katherine's eyes just as her gaze returned from the dancers, a bit of longing lingering in her expression.

Replacing his coffee cup, he debated his choices. He could ignore her feelings or he could be a gentleman. And, he reasoned, one dance couldn't hurt. ''Would you like to dance?''

Her eyes brightened, excitement filling her expression. "Oh, I'd love to."

Once on the smooth stone surface, Michael realized he hadn't thought out his impulsive offer. Putting his arms around her brought them suddenly only inches apart.

Katherine's hand was enclosed within his, her skin enticingly soft. And at the close proximity, he could smell the subtle spring-like aroma of her hair. Flowers and apples, he thought inanely.

Together they moved in unison to the music. For the second time since he'd met her he noticed her height, how it was a perfect complement to his own. For a moment he closed his eyes, briefly remembering the last time he'd danced, holding his petite wife in his arms. Nothing about Katherine reminded him of Ruth. From her irreverent sense of humor that seemed to encompass everything in life, to her physical appearance. It was all different. Very, very different.

But could different possibly be good?

When he'd first acknowledged that he was attracted to her, Michael had assumed it was because she *was* so different from his late wife...that a woman who resembled Ruth only would have been a painful reminder. But had that been a cop-out?

Was it instead because Katherine was Katherine, a tropical flower thriving amidst the native blooms?

She lifted her face, her brown eyes impossibly dark. And something in them pulled at him so strongly that it was almost a physical pain. Her lips were a gentle curve, one he wanted to explore.

And still the music swirled around them, romantically soft, evocative. When the song ended, neither of them pulled away.

As the second song started, Michael questioned his sanity. They began to dance again. His emotions were running high and it was neither comfort nor friendship he felt.

Katherine didn't exude a sense of homecoming…rather one of new exploration. And it had been a long time since he'd taken the first steps of such a journey.

Even if he were ready to start that journey, though, it couldn't be with a minister. He had convinced himself that he could reconcile his own beliefs to work on the church building. But he couldn't compromise his feelings to include dating someone who represented the source of his betrayal.

And this time when the music ended, he did pull back.

Surprise, followed by a flash of disappointment, crossed Katherine's face. Michael took her elbow, guiding her back to the table.

"I thought you might like some dessert," he attempted to explain, picking up his coffee cup, then replacing it in the saucer without drinking.

Her smile wasn't as broad as it had been. "I don't really feel like any, but you go ahead."

His stomach suddenly felt full of lead. "I think I'll just have coffee."

"Mmm," she murmured. But she didn't reach for her cup.

"Are you sure you don't want dessert? They're supposed to have a killer chocolate torte, and this *is* a thank-you dinner."

Her eyes flew up to meet his.

"For the—"

"Children," she completed his sentence flatly.

He started to correct her, to say it was for everything…for all of them, but the words wouldn't come. They couldn't. Because he was already too far over the line he'd drawn.

Chapter Ten

The stars truly were big and bright in Texas. At least, they seemed that way to Katherine. Despite the subdued ending to her dinner with Michael on Saturday night, she had put on her best smile and returned late on Monday afternoon to watch the children, allowing Mrs. Goode the time she still needed. Luckily, the older woman was able to spend a bit more time each day at the Carlson home. Her days freed, Katherine could still devote most evenings to David and Annie.

After all, Michael had made it clear that the dinner was only a thank-you between friends. Nothing more.

And the pain still fractured her.

Despite knowing she wasn't suited to be his wife, that she played too strong a role to fit in his traditional family, she had still held hidden hopes.

And now those were shattered.

Michael was late coming home, and she doubted it was a coincidence that he had managed to avoid dinner. She probably should have put the children to bed, but she had been drawn to the night sky as she often

was when troubled. After a few tales of her own star-
gazing times with her father, Annie and David had
become intrigued, begging to stay up.

They had carried two quilts out into the backyard,
snuggling on either side of her as they lay on their
backs, staring upward.

"I see more and more and more!" David exclaimed.

"They're all popping out!" Annie cried.

"I used to imagine that I could see them coming
out one at a time," Katherine confided.

"Can we count them?" David asked.

Katherine laughed. "You can try."

"I wish we could put them in a basket," Annie
told her. "It would be all shiny!"

"And that would be a beautiful basket, sweetie."

"You can't put stars in a basket," David scoffed.

"You're only as limited as your imagination,"
Katherine told him. "That's what opens up new vis-
tas, changes our world, makes it better."

"Do I have 'magnation?" Annie asked.

"Yes, you both do."

"Does Daddy have 'magnation?" Annie persisted.

Katherine swallowed her hurt. She had once
thought so.

"Of course." Michael's voice coming from the
dark surprised them all.

As Katherine sat up, the children scrambled to their
feet. "Daddy!"

"How are my stargazers?" he asked, after hugs
were exchanged.

"There's milk dippers in the sky," Annie told him.

"Big ones and little ones," David said with authority.

"I see," he replied seriously.

"And we're going to count all the stars," David told him.

"That should take a while," Michael responded with a mild smile.

"Katherine says with 'magnation we can do anything," Annie reported.

His gaze strayed to meet Katherine's. "Is that so?"

She lifted her head. "It's been my experience."

He sat down on the quilt next to Katherine's, and the children piled around them. "Then, I guess we ought to check out the sky, see what we can see."

"It's better if we lay down," David said, flinging himself on the quilt.

Obligingly Michael lay back. "It's funny. The stars are up there every night, but I can't remember when I looked at them last. When I was kid, we did this all the time."

"Katherine did, too!" David told him.

Michael angled his head, studying her. "Really?"

"I still do. It reminds me how infinite life is." She stopped short of saying *eternal,* but the unspoken inference lingered between them.

Michael spoke after a few moments. "My grandfather was somewhat of a naturalist, maybe the term is *environmentalist.* He made me aware of how we have to live in sync with nature, how important it is to conserve, that we have only one planet to experiment with. If we fail, it does too."

"That's why Daddy uses 'cycled stuff," Annie told her. "Even if it costs more."

"It's a good investment," Katherine replied. "One for *your* future, I'm sure."

"And well worth it," Michael agreed.

For a time they simply studied the stars, watching one errant cloud pass over the moon. When it cleared again, the children oohed at the sight.

But Katherine had lost her sense of comfort at the diversion. She was too aware of Michael's proximity…their last encounter. The deep dark of the night, the soft glow of the stars—all seemed to intensify the feelings.

So when Michael tapped her arm, she nearly bolted.

"Jumpy?" he asked.

Controlling her breathing with an effort, she tried to make her voice calm, her answer equally believable. "No. I was lulled by the exceptional quiet out here."

"Hmm." He didn't sound particularly believing as he continued. "So…which is your favorite constellation?"

"I like them all. Especially when they seem close enough to practically reach out and touch."

"Daddy, *they* think you can put stars in a basket," David told him in a loud whisper.

"Son, women are surprising creatures, with surprising abilities."

Startled, Katherine tried to hide her reaction. Just what did *that* mean?

But he didn't enlighten her further. Instead, they continued to study the stars, the crickets providing a nocturnal accompaniment. Shadows danced off the leaves that were caught in the glow of the outdoor lantern, and lush gardenias sweetened the air.

Katherine and Michael didn't speak. Instead, they longed for what could never be.

Her chest constricting, Katherine forced away the

threat of uncharacteristic tears. When she had offered to be only his friend, she hadn't realized what a difficult task that would be. Nor had she guessed how much Michael's rejection would hurt. It was for the best, she told herself, since she couldn't be the kind of wife he needed.

Yet the hurt resonated in the deep Texas night. And for the briefest moment she wondered why the Lord had led her to this path. But digging deep for strength, she knew He had never led her astray. And she had to trust He wasn't doing so now.

The following week was an emotionally difficult one for Michael, yet on Saturday he returned to the church to work on the repairs he'd promised to do. He needed the physical labor to clear his muddled thoughts.

His feelings for Katherine had progressed beyond his control. Yet he couldn't cross this final line. He couldn't embrace his faith...which was necessary to have a relationship with her. And he couldn't help wondering how she really felt. The night he'd held her in his arms as they danced, he'd suspected she might be feeling much as he did.

But her behavior since then hadn't indicated reciprocated emotions. Of course, he'd bungled the end of the evening terribly. Even though her smile had been back in place, it had never fully reached her eyes. Yet, if she didn't want to be anything more than friends, why was that so?

Wishing he had the answer, Michael searched for Katherine in her office, but it was vacant. Without her presence the room seemed dimmer somehow.

Reluctantly he entered the sanctuary, again feeling

the wash of conflicting emotions. How was it that the church offered such a sense of returning home after a lengthy and painful journey? Deep inside, he longed for that familiarity and anchor. Yet, in other ways, he still felt like a stranger, one who had been turned away. And although he stamped down the feelings, a persistent kernel inside longed for that haven.

Someone began playing the piano, an old-time spiritual he remembered from his childhood. And the lump in his throat told Michael the music of his youth could still move him. Unexpectedly, a voice added words to the song, a husky voice that tripped over him, evoking familiarity.

Walking slowly up the side aisle, he passed the pews without seeing them. The piano was angled so that the pianist was scarcely visible. Yet Michael knew who was singing. Katherine's distinctive voice was as recognizable as her wide grin and her refreshing sense of fun.

Her voice rose, echoing over the empty area. And he moved forward again. Katherine's head was bent over the music, her expression unfathomable. She was dressed simply, but the bright yellow of her T-shirt stood out against the subdued ivory walls.

The song drew to a close and the notes faded away.

"That was beautiful," he told her in a quiet voice.

Katherine's head jerked up, her expression unguarded, vulnerable. "I didn't know you were here."

He gestured to the tool belt secured around his waist. "I'm only halfway down your list of repairs."

"I shouldn't have asked you to do so many."

"Yes, you should have."

She didn't seem to have an answer, and the silence pulsed between them.

"I didn't know you sang," he said finally.

"Most of us have a few secrets," she replied.

Michael wasn't certain why, but he didn't believe she was referring to her musical talent. "Deep dark secrets?"

But her expression closed. "Not terribly."

Again he didn't believe her; however, her manner didn't invite speculation. "Oh."

When she didn't reply, another uncomfortable silence grew between them.

He couldn't quash the feeling that she was upset about something. "Are you okay, Katherine?"

"Any reason I shouldn't be?"

He swallowed, wondering at the cryptic reply. "If I've said something—"

"Of course not."

Sensing she would appreciate a change of topic, he reached for the handiest one. "I'm going to take a closer look at the wiring. Last week I was only able to make a cursory inspection. I'm a little worried since it's an old system."

Still looking distracted and somehow incredibly sad, she nodded. "It's been a source of concern in the past. But we haven't had the funds to bring in a contractor for evaluation."

"One of the advantages of having a contractor in your personal debt."

Another cloud passed over her face, then she smiled. "So it is."

Michael searched her expression for a moment before turning to walk away.

Katherine watched him, feeling her heart lodge in her throat. How had she allowed herself to be so completely swept up by this man and his life? Why hadn't she listened to logic? Why had she begun to hope that she might somehow escape her destiny?

Plagued by doubts, Katherine had been pondering whether she had irretrievably tangled the lines between her profession and her emotions. She should have been considering Michael's spiritual needs rather than her own personal ones, her role as his minister. Even though he kept insisting that she was *not* his minister, that he neither wanted nor needed a minister.

Debt had brought him to church today, but she could only hope that a return to faith would convince him to remain.

It had taken much prayer and soul-searching, but Katherine had come to the decision that she was ready to be the Lord's instrument. As much as it would hurt, she was willing to step away emotionally if it meant that Michael could find his way again.

Immediately, a picture of her parents' distressing breakup flashed through her thoughts. She could see her father's agony, the irreparable break in their family circle that had never healed. It was for the best, she told herself, that she wouldn't inflict the same fate on Michael, Annie and David.

Yet her heart wouldn't be still. Michael had crept inside, securing a foothold on emotions she had tried to contain. She admired that he didn't fit the mold of other men who had been intimidated by her job. Perhaps it was all the pain Michael had suffered in losing his wife, but intimidation wasn't his problem.

The gap that separated them, however, was far worse than intimidation. And far more impossible to bridge.

* * *

Frowning, Michael closed the church's fuse box. The repairs he'd made had only reinforced his earlier suspicions. Walking up the short half flight of stairs, he crossed the hall toward Katherine's office. She sat at her desk, absorbed by whatever she was writing on her computer. Still unaware of his presence, she wrinkled her brow, then smiled as she typed rapidly.

Although he didn't want to admit it, she took his breath away. Her long hair was loose, draping over her shoulders. Late-afternoon sun glinted on the dark waves, a teasing play of light. Even sitting at her desk, she radiated energy. She had fire, Michael realized, fire in her soul. And despite the contradiction, he realized that was what attracted him to her, drew him as no other woman had.

She glanced up just then, her mahogany-colored eyes deepening to an even darker hue. Again he sensed a wealth of hidden secrets, and now, even more strongly, wondered why.

"Hi." She greeted him.

"You looked glued to that screen. Something interesting?"

She met his gaze. "I hope so. It's tomorrow's sermon. Come and listen. Then you can judge its quality for yourself."

Immediately his defenses leaped to attention. "I'll take your word for it."

"Actually," she countered, "Annie has a part in the program tomorrow. I'm sure she'd love to see you there supporting her."

At a Sunday morning service. No...he couldn't.

"She's singing with the other young Sunday

School classes, and her teacher tells me Annie has a solo.''

He groaned inwardly. What a choice. Enter the source of his betrayal or fail to support his daughter. Why was it Katherine kept pushing? Couldn't she just leave well enough alone, let him deal with his beliefs in his own way? ''Should I ask whose idea it was for the solo?''

Katherine shrugged but met his gaze evenly. ''I wasn't part of the selection process, if that's what you mean. But if I have to venture a guess, I'd say it was because she has a remarkably sweet voice. Surely you've noticed.''

Had he lately? Michael wondered. It seemed he spent every waking moment keeping home and body together.

When he didn't answer, she seemed to sense his quandary. ''So, how are the repairs going?''

''I've had time to thoroughly examine the church building.''

''And?''

''I'm afraid the repairs I've made are only a stop-gap measure. The roof must be replaced. And the building itself needs major structural renovation and restoration.''

Although her brows drew together, she nodded.

''Worse, the antiquated wiring is a serious threat. You've been fortunate that the church hasn't suffered any damage, but you can't be lucky forever. Frankly, the wiring's downright scary.''

Again she nodded. ''Then, we'll have to take care of the problems.''

He realized she probably knew little about construction or repair costs. A new wiring system didn't come cheap. "Katherine, I don't think you understand the scope of what I'm talking about. It's going to be extremely expensive."

Her expression was unruffled. "God will provide."

Michael cleared his throat rather than make a harsh comment. He knew from experience that wasn't true. "In the meantime, you'd better check out all your fire extinguishers—make sure they're all in tiptop shape."

She frowned. "Is the problem that serious?"

"I don't want to scare you. The building's been around for a lot of years and chances are it will survive for many more. But don't get complacent. You need to start on the repairs as soon as possible."

"I'll meet with the church board on Monday. I'm sure they'll share your concern."

"Good." For a moment he hesitated, wondering if he dared ask her to another dinner. After the last one, he wasn't too confident of a different outcome.

But Katherine spoke before he could. "In the meantime, I hope you'll reconsider attending church tomorrow. I'm sure your presence would mean the world to Annie."

Her words hit him like a bucket of cold water. Dinner was a foolhardy idea, as was any time spent alone with Katherine. "Why don't you let me worry about that?"

But she didn't try to cajole him; her expression remained sober. "You have to face it sometime, Michael."

Maybe so, but Katherine wasn't going to call the shots. A picture of his daughter's trusting face flashed through his thoughts. And Michael wished he didn't have to call the shots, either.

Chapter Eleven

The following morning the church was hushed. Only the sound of lowered voices broke the quiet. The service would begin in a few minutes, yet Michael shifted for the dozenth time on the well-padded pew. He still couldn't believe he was sitting in the sanctuary. It had been different coming in to do repairs. He had been able to reason that it was simply work, nothing to do with the Lord. But now, sitting in His house, the rationale wasn't easy to maintain.

Annie's pleas had worn him down. He couldn't find an answer when she'd asked him why he didn't care about her song. The expression on her sweet face told him she was brokenhearted. And he'd crumbled. Late the previous evening he had reasoned that he could simply attend, keep his distance and not allow his surroundings to affect him.

But that wasn't the case. Thousands of memories assailed him. Good ones—like the many times he had sat beside his parents, confident in the belief that all was right with the world.

And then there were the dark memories. Ones of betrayed trust, pain and disbelief. Disbelief that something he believed in so strongly had failed him.

As the service progressed, Michael tried to shove away the memories. But the minutes ticked by slowly. And the memories, both good and bad, continued to assault him.

Finally the Sunday School classes rose from the front rows to stand on the steps at the front of the pulpit. Despite his resistance, Michael swelled with pride when he gazed at his son and daughter. Young voices blended together as they sang "Jesus Loves Me."

Consulting his program, Michael knew that the second selection, "Gladly the Cross I Bear," was Annie's solo. It was only one verse, but Michael had spent most of the previous evening helping her practice. She thought the words were "Gladly the Cross-Eyed Bear."

While Michael expected that rendition would produce a ripple of laughter in the congregation, he didn't want Annie hurt. She had told him that her teacher had instructed her to rely on the Lord for help when she needed it. And in her usual caring way, Annie had told him not to worry, that she would remember the right words.

With her teacher prompting her, Annie stepped forward. Her high, sweet voice began delivering the verse. Michael's pride multiplied. At the same time, his heart was touched and he tried to tell himself it had nothing to do with the Lord.

But the thought was fading as Annie sang, sweet and true. Love and pride mixing, Michael's throat worked as he was flooded by emotions.

The song drew to a close, and the children filed off the podium. Michael had planned to leave as soon as that portion of the service concluded, but he saw Annie heading directly toward him. David was only a few steps behind.

Trapped, he waited as his children slipped in to sit beside him. He squeezed Annie's shoulder, signaling his pleasure at her solo. Her answering smile was instant and huge.

Katherine stepped behind the pulpit, and he stiffened.

After a few preliminary words, she glanced at him. Was it his imagination that she was singling him out?

"I would like to extend a warm Rosewood welcome to those of you who have chosen to visit with us for the first time today."

His irritation ignited, and Michael knew his imagination was not overacting.

"I encourage our members to stand and greet both our visitors and one another," she continued.

It took a few seconds, but Michael realized that although her words *were* directed at him, it was a personal welcome, one he didn't have to share with the rest of the congregation.

As he remained seated, several people offered congenial welcomes. It wasn't nearly as painful as standing alone to be gawked at.

His irritation receded but he couldn't quite put a name to the emotion that followed when her sermon began. Her topic was on forgiveness and trust...trust in the Lord even when we don't understand His purpose.

Neither her design nor the irony escaped him. Even though he resented the choice of topics, he couldn't suppress his admiration at her style and delivery. The enthusiasm she gave to everyday events absolutely poured from the pulpit. Again he realized what she gave the congregation—her fire.

After the service ended, Michael shepherded the children toward the exit. Katherine greeted each member by name, clearly enjoying this aspect of her job.

When she met his gaze she hesitated for only a moment. "I'm pleased you joined us, Michael."

He nodded, his gaze cutting to his children, letting her know he wouldn't say anything disparaging in front of them.

"How did you judge the sermon?" she continued.

One lip curled. "It's not my place to judge—however, I'd be extremely interested in knowing when you chose the subject."

Her lip twitched, as well. "I think that comes under pastoral discretion." Then she bent to greet the children.

Annie impulsively flung her arms around Katherine's neck. "Did you like my song?"

"It was wonderful, sweetie." Her glance moved to include David. "You both did a spectacular job."

"You, too," the forthright boy replied. "Guess we all did."

Katherine chuckled. "Thanks! I guess we did." Her gaze lifted to meet Michael's. "So, what fun things are you doing this afternoon?"

Annie and David both shrugged. Michael, however, stiffened. He didn't want to be put into the position of refusing an invitation to the church picnic. "We don't have any specific plans."

"Sometimes a lazy day is best," Katherine replied, surprising him.

"Daddy reads us the comics," David told her. "There's lots on Sundays."

"One of the many benefits of the Lord's day," she replied easily.

Cautiously Michael nodded, ready to end the exchange.

"Oh, there is one thing," she said, as he took a step to move away.

He knew it! If she thought she would push him into another picnic he couldn't refuse—

"The kids told me that you used to play softball."

Thrown, he tried to guess her new motive. "Yes. It's been a while, though."

"We play on Tuesday evenings, and we're short a player. We could really use you this week. We're playing the church from Schlumberg, and they have a killer team."

"You could play, Daddy!" Annie exclaimed.

"Yeah. You could show 'em how good you are," David added.

"Please!" they cried in unison.

Helplessly he glanced between his children and Katherine. Was her smile a tad *too* beatific?

"I'm not sure," he tried to protest. "I'll have the kids and—"

"They're welcome, too. And we'll have hot dogs and lemonade."

"Please, Daddy!" they cried again.

"You'd really be helping us," Katherine added to the mix.

He knew it was time to gracefully acquiesce. After

all, softball wasn't played inside the church. "I suppose it won't kill me *this once*."

She acknowledged his emphasis, then smiled. "Probably not. But I guess we'll see on Tuesday."

Startled, his gaze flew to hers. Then he spotted the laughter lurking in her eyes. Despite his resistance, he couldn't help grinning. "Wouldn't do much for your church's reputation if you knocked off your players."

Her answering smile was uncomfortably captivating. "You got me there."

He didn't, but it worried him that the prospect was so appealing.

Sunshine warmed the late August afternoon. Bright glinting light bounced between both softball teams. Katherine adjusted her ball cap, allowing her ponytail to escape through the back opening.

She hated to admit how much she'd looked forward to the game. Mrs. Goode had switched mornings for afternoons the previous week, and Katherine hadn't seen much of Michael other than at church when he worked on the repairs, and for those brief moments on Sunday. And that time hadn't lent itself to private conversation.

She closed her eyes now, remembering her resolution. Remembering that she couldn't hope to be any more to him than a friend.

Then he sauntered onto the field, and the resolution fled her thoughts, scattered her emotions.

"Hello, Coach," he greeted her.

"I'm just one of the players," she corrected him. "I'm not good enough to be the coach."

"Don't listen to her." Tom Sanders spoke up from

behind her. A sandy-haired, perpetually smiling man, he was the coach of their team. "She's better than any other two players we have."

"Better not let your team overhear," Michael responded with a grin, "or you'll be more than one player short."

Tom extended his hand. "You must be our pinch hitter."

"And you must be overly optimistic," Michael responded.

Tom chuckled. "You'll fit in just fine on our team." His gaze cut over to Katherine. "She said you would."

Katherine smiled at Michael, hoping he didn't think she'd rattled on about his private life. Out of the corner of her eye she spotted Cindy, and her hopes sank. As much as she loved her best friend, Cindy could chatter, and was capable of revealing far more than Katherine wished. Her only hope was that Cindy would keep on walking past them.

Instead, her friend veered in their direction, heading straight toward the team.

"Hi, all!" Cindy greeted them. Her gaze immediately zeroed in on Michael. "I know everybody here except you. Anyone want to correct that?"

Katherine cleared her throat, but Michael was already extending his hand. "Michael Carlson."

"Cindy Thompson," she replied, dragging her eyes from Michael over to Katherine and then back again. "So, have you come to play with us?"

Katherine sent her friend a pleading glance.

Cindy smiled in return, her brows rising in appreciation as she studied Michael.

"Do you want us to take our positions to warm up, Tom?" Katherine asked desperately.

Tom shrugged. "I'm not sure that'll help. I've watched Schlumberg's team play before. Unless they're all incapacitated with the flu, I'm afraid we're doomed."

Katherine tried again. "You haven't seen Michael play yet."

"Whoa," Michael protested. "No expectations, please."

Cindy casually linked her arm with Michael's. "If Katherine and Tom want to practice, let them. I'll keep you company."

Michael glanced toward the hot dog stand. "I need to keep an eye on my kids."

"I'm sure Katherine will do that," Cindy replied breezily, guiding him toward the bleachers. As she left, she looked back over her shoulder, winking at Katherine.

It was clear what Cindy was up to. She wanted time to push Michael and Katherine together. Katherine nearly groaned aloud, wondering how she could convince her friend to stop.

"Katherine," Tom repeated, sounding concerned.

She pulled her attention back. "I'm sorry. I'm kind of distracted. What did you say?"

"I was suggesting that if you want to warm up, we need to get out on the field."

"If you think we must."

Tom's usually smiling face was a bit exasperated. "It was *your* idea."

So it was.

She took one last longing glance toward the bleachers, then sighed. She could hardly tell Tom she wanted to rescue Michael from Cindy's too, too helpful clutches.

Annie and David, loaded with hot dogs and drinks, waved to her. She ran over and made sure they were seated near one of the women in the church who had promised to keep an eye on them.

The pre-game warm-up crawled by with excruciating slowness. When Cindy and Michael finally strolled back to the field, Katherine's anxiety level was topped out.

Michael, however, seemed at ease, as he began tossing the ball back and forth with Tom.

Katherine tried not to stare but it was difficult. How was it that Michael looked so handsome in shorts and a simple T-shirt? And how was it that it had become so difficult to focus on anything other than him?

One of the other players had run out on the field, and was talking excitedly with Tom. Curious, Katherine joined them. She was just in time to hear Tom's woeful words.

"Great. No pitcher. We won't just lose, we'll be smeared."

"Is anything seriously wrong with Gregg?" she questioned, concerned.

"No. Emergency business trip. Gregg's sorry, but he can't make the game."

"So, who's going to pitch?" Katherine asked.

Tom shrugged. "I suppose I can give it try." Then his gaze sharpened. "Unless our new recruit has had some pitching experience."

Michael demurred. "Hey, I haven't pitched in a long time. I'm sure you can find someone more qualified."

"Afraid not. Gregg was our only pitcher."

Michael glanced at Katherine, and she wondered if he thought she'd dreamed up this scenario to push him into becoming more involved with the team. "I can give it a try. But don't expect much."

Both teams got into position. Katherine tried not to stare at Michael, but then reasoned she should be paying attention to her team's pitcher. Somehow, the excuse sounded weak even to her.

Play began. Michael threw two balls, and inwardly Katherine groaned. She didn't want him embarrassed after being roped in first to play, then to substitute as pitcher. But his third pitch was a strike. As were the following two.

Excitement began to stir on the Rosewood team. But was the accomplishment a fluke?

The next batter was up. Michael's first pitch was a ball. Then a strike. And another. A ball followed, but so did another strike.

New life infused the Rosewood team. Katherine found herself grinning. Since she played first base, she was in direct line with Michael and she could see that he was pleased. She hoped he felt a sense of camaraderie with the team. She suspected fellowship was only one of many things he missed about church.

As the game progressed, Rosewood stayed ahead of the competition. Katherine made several base hits, and Michael struck gold with two home runs.

By the end of the ninth inning, their team had won, and was giddy with unaccustomed success. Surrounding Michael, they insisted on taking him and his children out for pizza. He couldn't refuse without offending them. And in seconds Michael was swept into their good cheer.

Watching him, Katherine's heart was warmed by the fellowship her friends were offering.

At the pizza place, Annie and David sought her out, each catching one of her hands. So it was natural for her to sit beside Michael at the tables the team had pushed together. She and Michael were at the core of the group, and she couldn't help thinking this was much the way life would be if they could overcome their barriers.

It made the moment bittersweet…the wondering, the wishing…the wanting.

As that instant, Michael raised his eyes, meeting hers.

Did she imagine the longing she glimpsed there?

"Michael, you're drafted," Tom announced, breaking the connection. "We definitely want you on our team."

It looked for a second as though Michael wouldn't address the comment, then reluctantly he turned his attention to the other man. "I have a pretty full schedule already."

"But you're first rate. You've got to allow some time for softball."

Michael's gaze drifted again toward Katherine. "I'm not sure I can commit right now."

She swallowed, a thousand questions stirring in her mind.

"You'll find we don't give up easily," Tom persisted.

Again Michael's gaze nailed Katherine's. "So I've learned."

Something inexplicable gripped her. And again she felt the sharp thrust of connection. A tenuous one perhaps, but one that seemed to single them out from the crowd.

Tom clapped Michael's shoulder. "We have another game on Friday. If you don't show up, we'll come collect you."

Since the words were delivered with admiration, Michael was able to grin in response.

Then Tom's face screwed up in concentration. "Say, are you the Michael who's been doing the repairs at the church?"

"That would be me."

"Ah."

Katherine saw the questions on Michael's face and spoke quickly, again not wanting him to think she'd spoken out of turn about him. "Tom's on the board. We met yesterday to discuss the repairs."

"Sounds like it'll cost a lot of money," Tom mused.

"It will," Michael responded. "The necessary repairs are extensive."

"Unfortunately, our funds aren't—" Tom bemoaned.

"Which is why we've applied for a bank loan," Katherine broke in.

"I thought you said the Lord would provide," Michael replied quietly, as Tom turned his attention to the man on his other side.

"He has many ways of providing," she responded.

"You're so sure?"

She met his eyes. "As sure as I am that the sun will set each night and rise again in the morning."

"And what if it doesn't?"

Immediately she recognized the meaning of Michael's seemingly unreasonable question. "Even on the darkest days, it's there. Sometimes it's hiding deep behind the thickest clouds as though it's been vanquished, but it's still giving life.''

The pain in his eyes deepened. ''I've stood in the cold, waiting for the warmth, but it never came.''

She wanted so much to lend her strength, even a fraction of her faith. ''That's when it's hardest to believe.''

''You're wrong, Katherine. That's when it's easiest to believe.''

There was no answer, no explanation, no comforting words. Nothing she could think of to remove the anguish in his eyes. And she knew the anguish was far deeper than the loss of his wife. It was the loss of his faith.

Chapter Twelve

A week later Tom frowned as he read the bank's preliminary report. Absently he passed the cream to Katherine, then pushed back his chair a fraction. "Sounds like we're going to have to spend a mint for a structural report before we even know if the bank's going to give us the loan."

Katherine's brows drew together as she placed the creamer on the table without adding any to her coffee. "Maybe not."

Tom lifted his gaze from the papers. "You have an idea?"

"I'm not sure. I'm hoping perhaps we can get one for a reasonable amount."

Tom's gaze narrowed. "From our star pitcher?"

Flustered, she tried to think of a reply.

Tom saved her the effort. "Relax, Katherine, you told me he was doing the repairs at the church." Then his eyes softened. "Hey, it's okay for the preacher to have someone special in her life."

Troubled, she couldn't quite meet his gaze. "It's not that simple."

"You know, I've been on the church board for a lot of years, and I've seen quite a few preachers at our pulpit. In fact, I was one of the diehards who thought only a man should have that particular position. Then I met you, Katherine. And you've changed my mind about that and more. But I'm still certain about one aspect—things are only as complicated as you make them. For laypeople *and* preachers."

Katherine thought about his words as they completed their meeting, then as the afternoon wore on. Could he be right? Had she made things more complicated than they needed to be? And hadn't she once made the same observation to Michael?

The afternoon turned to evening. Michael phoned to say he wouldn't be able to make the softball game. So Katherine had taken David and Annie along to watch her play. They had happily stuffed themselves with hot dogs and lemonade. To her delight, Pastor James McPherson and his wife had stopped by on their return to Houston from a trip for seminary business. The McPhersons and the Carlson children had taken to one another instantly.

In fact, James had commented that Katherine was a natural with the kids. His remark pleased her, but she couldn't dismiss the belief that baby-sitting was far different than motherhood. Still, she was unable to shake the image of James's wise and knowing expression. Could there be any truth to his words?

She had replayed them as she spent the evening with Annie and David. Now, despite their protests, the kids were finally asleep upstairs. And still Katherine was mulling over James's words. Combined with Tom's advice, it was quite a lot to think about.

Hearing the back door open, Katherine stood and crossed to the kitchen, relieved Michael was home safe. She had begun to worry.

"Sorry I'm so late," he began. "We had some serious complications at the site today. For a while I thought we might have been set back irreparably."

"Did you solve the problems?"

He pulled off his cap, crossed to the sink and began washing his hands. "I think so. We'll know tomorrow when we find out if we got approval from the zoning commission."

"Good."

Wiping his hands, Michael glanced at his watch. "It's really late. You sure you're not ready to bail?"

She shook her head. "It's not in my makeup."

He paused. "No. I don't suppose it is." He moved a few steps closer. "But I feel terrible about keeping you here so late. Is there anything I can do to make it up to you?"

Katherine clasped her hands together. "Funny you should ask."

He raised his eyebrows. "What is it?"

"Actually we need a structural report before the bank will consider our improvement loan."

"You got it."

Surprised, she studied his face. "Just like that? Don't you want to discuss the price?"

"Nope. There won't be a price. I can't ever repay you for taking care of the kids. Even with the report, I'll still be in your debt."

"But I understand these reports cost thousands. I was only hoping for a price break."

"Nope," he repeated. "I don't think you grasp how much it means to me to know my children are safe and well cared for. You can't put a price on that. Just like I won't put a price on your report."

"But—"

"No arguments. I'll start on it tomorrow."

She bit her lip.

"Are you worried about what I'll find?"

"Somewhat."

"I thought you said the Lord would provide."

"I've no doubt He will," she replied quietly. "That's never a question for me."

"Then, you're lucky," he responded, unable to hide his bitterness.

"No. I'm blessed. And that's far better than luck."

Blessed. The following afternoon Michael still doubted that. Unless being blessed meant that your historical church building failed its structural report. Strangely, being right didn't please him. In fact, he hated to pass on this news to Katherine. He'd learned that the church funds were sparse. And without the bank loan, they were sunk.

Katherine was at home with his children. He called, asking her to set the backyard table for dinner, knowing the kids would be easily distracted by the trampoline. He also told her he was bringing pizza, a sure-fire way to keep David occupied.

He had to break the news to Katherine gently. Michael wasn't certain why that was so important to him, but he didn't want to examine his reasons. He only knew that he didn't want to hurt this very special woman.

Katherine and the kids were weeding in the garden,

when he stepped into the yard. Vibrant yellow and green peppers, their glossy skins shining in the late-afternoon sun, flourished next to ripening tomatoes and tall stalks of corn. Marigolds, petunias, daisies and moss roses flanked the vegetables, lending more hues to the colorful display. The once sadly neglected corner now pulsed with new life and purpose. Much as he and his family had since Katherine had entered their lives, Michael realized.

"Pizza man," he called out, not wanting to dwell on that last thought.

The kids came running. After hugs were exchanged, they were happy to carry the pizza to the table.

Michael snagged Katherine's arm, pulling her out of earshot.

"Is something wrong?" she asked, concern filling her expression.

He wished suddenly for better news. "It's the structural report."

"Have you finished it already?"

He hesitated.

"You have, haven't you?"

"I'm afraid so."

"What is it, Michael?"

"It's not good. Based on what I've found, I doubt the bank will grant the loan."

Her expression sagged. "Are you sure?"

"There's no question. And I can't cut corners on the report. Structural integrity—rather the loss of it—could cost lives."

"I agree." Her eyes lightened. "Don't worry. During the services tomorrow, we'll pray for assistance. I know God will provide."

Her insistence amazed him. She was facing losing the church, yet she didn't budge an inch in her faith. For a fleeting moment, he yearned for the security of faith, one he'd once worn like a protective blanket. One that even now beckoned to him. "You're so sure?"

She laid her hand on his arm, her eyes imploring. "As sure as I am that you'll find your way again."

Bitter yearning clogged his emotions. "And if I don't?"

Something unfathomable deepened in her eyes, something resembling love, but then it was quickly masked. And he supposed he'd imagined that fleeting glimpse. Had he wanted to see into her heart so much that he'd conjured up the look in her eyes? Given substance to something that existed only in his dreams?

But she didn't linger to allow him to confirm or deny his suspicions, instead walking quickly to the table, shuttering her thoughts.

The following Wednesday, Katherine sat beside Tom in the bank manager's office.

Loren Johnson glanced from one to the other sympathetically. "I'm really sorry, but based on the structural report, we can't extend the financing."

Katherine swallowed, trying to make her smile bright. "It's not like we're going to run out on the loan."

"I know you aren't. But I answer to my board, Katherine. And based on this report, you don't have enough collateral to secure a repair loan."

"But surely the building itself is collateral," Katherine argued.

Loren's face was sympathetic. "According to the structural evaluation, the entire building may be a loss."

Not expecting that, Katherine sucked in a deep breath of disbelief.

Tom patted her arm reassuringly, but he, too, looked shocked. "Are you sure, Loren?"

The manager nodded. "I'm afraid so. In fact I've gone over the report several times, looking for another answer. Unfortunately, there's no way we can grant the loan."

Dismayed, Katherine managed to thank the man. Then she and Tom left the bank.

"This is worse news than I expected," Tom said, still reeling.

"I needed some fresh air," Katherine murmured, sinking back against the brick exterior.

"We need more than that," Tom muttered, still looking shell-shocked.

"The Lord will provide," Katherine assured him.

"I know. I just hope it's before the building falls down."

Michael noticed that Katherine had been uncharacteristically quiet. It was something that had been happening frequently over the past few days.

"Did you hear from the bank?"

"We met with the manager today."

"Bad news?"

"They aren't going to give us the loan."

"I thought you said the Lord would provide."

"I said the Lord would provide, not the bank," she pointed out gently. "And He will."

Amazed, Michael stared at her. "And you still believe that?"

"Absolutely. My faith hasn't wavered. My prayers may not have been answered as I thought they would, but I know they were heard."

"Maybe they'll be answered as mine were," he replied ironically, not wishing that fate on her but knowing how likely it was.

"Perhaps." She met his gaze. "But that won't affect my faith. I haven't always received the answer I hoped for, but I can't imagine how empty my life would be without Him."

As empty as mine, Michael acknowledged. Yet he couldn't let go of the bitterness…the betrayal.

Katherine laid a tentative hand on his arm. "You may not believe this but I've been disappointed, too, about some of my own answers. I think most everyone has. It's awfully hard for us mere mortals to understand the entire scope of the heavens and our place in it."

Meeting her eyes, he glimpsed traces of pain she couldn't quite hide. He wasn't certain why, but he didn't believe the sorrow was related to the loss of the bank loan. "Katherine, what has hurt you?"

For a moment her eyes shimmered and her lips trembled ever so slightly. Then she averted her face. "My mind's just full right now. As you pointed out, we don't have a bank loan or much hope of getting one."

"You don't believe that," he replied, startling himself.

"What I do believe is that the Lord is always with me," she replied. Then she stood. "But I'd better get home and start thinking about some fund-raisers."

"Don't go," he protested. "It's still early."

Her still saddened gaze traveled toward Annie and David, who were playing in the fading twilight. "Without me, you'll be able to spend some family time together...the most valuable time."

Turning, she fled.

Although he stood to object, Katherine didn't glance back, instead disappearing into the dusk. And as he tried to figure out what had just gone wrong, Michael realized just how much he'd come to count on her presence. And how much he would miss her if she continued to pull away.

The swings and slide weren't the only attractions in the park. At least, not for Michael. In the park the kids were occupied by the amusements, allowing Michael time alone with Katherine. And it was time he desperately needed. More than a week had passed, and Michael still didn't know why Katherine was so quiet, why she continued to withdraw. Each day in so many small ways she was distancing herself. And he neither knew why...nor knew how he could stop it.

"You haven't told me. How's the fund-raising coming for the repairs?"

Distracted, she frowned slightly. "Kind of slow."

Immediately he thought of the precarious wiring system. He wouldn't want Katherine to be working in her office if it failed. And he refused to examine the rightness of that thought. "Katherine, the repairs really can't wait. It's only a matter of time, and maybe not much of it, until the wiring shorts out and starts a fire."

Worry creased her expression. "But if it's lasted

all this time, won't it hang together until we get the money?''

He wished he could reassure her. "I'm afraid not. It's nothing short of a miracle that the whole place hasn't gone up like a stack of dry kindling."

She dissected his words. "At least you admit there *are* miracles."

"It's just an expression."

But she waved away his explanation. "No. It's not. The Lord's protecting us and that *is* a miracle."

"For your sake, I hope that lasts. But on a practical basis, you're literally playing with fire. Just a routine test of the fuse box causes more sparks than you'd need for it to combust."

"We could stop testing it," she suggested.

"Won't do any good to hide your head in the sand," he rebuked her gently.

"Did you know ostriches really don't do that?" she questioned, blatantly changing the subject. "It's a misconception. It's simply a defensive stance they take near their nests to camouflage and protect the eggs."

"Katherine, avoiding the issue won't make it go away."

She sighed. "I don't suppose I really want it to go away. We just haven't come up with a good solution to find the money. We've organized a bake sale, and our carnival's scheduled for the beginning of September. They'll be a start, and even if they only bring in a small amount, the Lord will show us the way."

"And what if He doesn't?"

Her smile was tender yet knowing. "My faith isn't a pick-and-choose proposition. It's there no matter what."

As his used to be. Unable to still the motion, he reached out, catching her hand. "Katherine, you might not be safe there."

She stared at their joined hands, slowly raising her eyes to meet his. "That's where you're wrong. It's the only place I *am* safe."

It seemed her words left far more unsaid than expressed, and he wondered why that was. Also, why her huge eyes were filled with a knowing pain. From sensation in the pit of his stomach, he guessed she would withdraw even farther. And there wasn't a solitary thing he could do to prevent it.

Small towns like Rosewood seemed made for carnivals. Old oak trees thrived because they didn't have to be cut down to make room for new buildings. And those trees provided a natural canopy for the booths and games that lined the perimeter of the church parking lot. A cotton-candy machine whirled nonstop, adding the sweet smell of scorched sugar to the aroma of hot dogs and popcorn. The fragrance of grilled knockwurst and bratwurst tantalized taste buds for blocks.

Dominating the center of the carnival, the haunted house was a huge draw, eliciting delighted screams and groans. It was designed to appeal to kids and teens alike, so it wasn't too scary. But scary enough that David and Annie asked to go through twice.

Michael kept searching the crowd for Katherine, but there were more people in attendance than he'd expected. He had thought it would be a quiet, intimate affair, one at which he could talk to Katherine. To his surprise, apparently most of the town had turned out for the annual event.

Then he felt a familiar touch on his arm. Turning, he met Katherine's grin.

"So what do you think of our little carnival?"

He laughed, enjoying the mischievous look on her face. "You could have told me it was the biggest draw in town."

"And ruin the surprise?" She glanced around. "Where are David and Annie?"

He pointed to a game close by. "Playing ring toss for the sixth or seventh time."

"I hope everyone will. It'll help fill the repair coffers."

"Do you think you'll make enough from the carnival to get started on the restoration?"

She shrugged. "It's a good fund-raiser, but we don't usually make a huge amount. We keep the prices low so everyone can afford to attend. For big families, especially, it's one of the few events they can truly afford."

"Admirable, but it won't get you a new wiring system."

"I believe you're more worried about that than I am."

"*I* saw the system," he pointed out. "Which makes me glad the carnival's running on a generator."

She looked puzzled. "Does that make a difference?"

"It keeps from overloading your already overloaded circuits."

She bit her lip.

Wary, he met her gaze. "Katherine?"

"Well, we don't actually have a generator."

"*What?*"

"There wasn't enough money in our budget. We're running extension cords."

Appalled, he stared at her. "Katherine! That's dangerous!"

She fidgeted. "Now that you've pointed out the generator issue, I can see that."

"You need to shut everything down, *now!*"

"Oh, we can't! Everyone has worked so hard and looked forward to the carnival!" Her voice grew coaxing. "Besides, we've had this same carnival every year. We haven't had a problem before."

"You haven't had a leak directly into the wiring system before, either!" he retorted. "Water from your leaky roof has exacerbated the problem."

Shifting uncomfortably, Katherine looked apologetic. "I appreciate your expertise and concern, but I really think everything will be all right. I'll keep a close watch on things."

"Better do it with a fire extinguisher in hand," he replied in exasperation.

"I will," she promised. "Actually, I bought a new extinguisher after we talked the first time."

"It's a step, Katherine, but only a small one."

"Sometimes those are the only kind of steps we *can* take." She reached out, laying her hand on his arm. "Please don't worry, Michael. Everything will be fine."

He paused, but guessed nothing he could say would convince her. Instead he sighed. "If I can't convince you, then how about coming with me to the booths?"

Her hesitation was barely perceptible. "Fine. Should we collect the kids?"

"Sure. They should be tiring of ring toss by now."

With Annie and David flanking them, they visited

the stalls that boasted everything from fine art to toys made from yarn and wood. But it was at one of the last booths that Michael's eyes lit up.

Distracting Katherine, he sent her with the kids to buy snow cones. His idea might seem a silly gesture, but he guessed she would like it.

His purchase complete, Michael caught up with them. Katherine's hand was filled with a large snow cone, and a bit of the strawberry syrup had found its way onto her cheek. Somehow, it looked perfect there. Just as she did.

She looked up, met his eyes, and he felt something deep inside solidify. Refusing to dwell on the feeling, he held out his gift.

Katherine blinked, stared, then blinked again. "A giant bubble blower?"

"You said you blew killer bubbles." He couldn't voice the reason behind the impulsive gesture, his desire to see the pleasure in her expression. "Now you can prove it."

For a moment her eyes glistened suspiciously. "You remembered," she murmured. Then a wide, if tremulous, smile reached across her face as she held up the two-foot hoop. "Thank you."

Annie and David were immediately entranced with the huge bubble blower. "Can we help?"

She glanced at them fondly. "I was hoping you'd offer."

Michael glanced at the trio, thinking again how right they seemed together.

And Katherine *could* blow killer bubbles. Enormous, iridescent rings of soap that took on mystical proportions as they floated skyward.

David and Annie teamed together to blow through

the large hoop, thrilling as a mammoth bubble burst forth.

"We did it!" David exclaimed.

"I knew you could!" Katherine exulted, giving him a hug.

"That's the bestest present," Annie told her.

Katherine's eyes lifted toward Michael. "Yes. It is. The bestest one I ever got."

Again something warmed inside, and Michael realized it felt right. All of it. Himself, Katherine and his children. Unbelievably right.

Chapter Thirteen

Katherine wasn't sure what woke her. It could have been the blanket of smoke that crept insidiously through the windows she had opened to allow the sweet autumn air to enter. Or possibly the frantic barking of her dog. Or it could have been the *clang* of the fire engine sirens breaking the quiet of the night.

Bolting upright, Katherine's heartbeat stampeded out of control. She threw on clothes, grabbing the nearest ones she could find. Dashing through the house, she flung open her front door, not bothering to close it as she ran outside. Snowy was at her side, barking furiously, nipping at her heels, urging her to flee.

For a moment she stood paralyzed, watching as the flames leaped up the steeple, greedily consuming the dry, aged timber. Flames from the chapel shot up in the air like a grotesque bonfire, singeing the ancient oaks and smothered the surrounding buildings.

She wasn't certain when the tears came. It could

have been as she found her feet and tore off toward the church. Or later when it was clear all hope to save the building was gone.

Hours after it began, fire trucks remained sprawled across the street, the hoses a giant jumble. Firemen covered each portion of the church property, spraying water on the ruined building. Persistent embers stirred despite the massive onslaught.

A television crew from a larger nearby town stayed long enough to record some quick and shocking images to fill the morning news hour. But Katherine couldn't be persuaded to give a comment. The loss was too personal to be reduced to a sound bite.

Irrespective of the damage beneath it, the sun rose, clear strong beams that illuminated the smoke-blackened stone, the soggy ash debris...the complete devastation.

As they had all night, people remained grouped around the church. It was a sober gathering.

"Such a shame," one person sympathized. "That building's been here as long as the town."

"Yes," Katherine agreed, to this stranger to whom the loss was nothing more than historical interest.

Members of the church felt compelled to share their tears and sorrow, though, looking to her even now for leadership. And all Katherine could think of were Michael's words—his warning.

Then someone was pulling her into a hug. But it couldn't be, could it?

"Michael?" she whispered against his shoulder, craving the solace of his embrace.

"I heard about it on the news." He pulled back slightly, offering her an encouraging smile. "Before I had my coffee. It was enough to wake me up."

"It is that," she agreed almost tonelessly.

"I'm sorry, Katherine."

"Me, too. I should have listened to you."

He stared at her in disbelief. "You're not blaming yourself for this, are you?"

"You told me what could happen, and I didn't listen."

"God failed you, Katherine. Don't you see that?"

"It's not His fault. It's mine."

"How can you say that? Everything you've trusted in is in rubble at your feet!"

Pain scissored across her face, but she didn't waver. "Faith can't be rubble. And I'm sorry you don't see that. I had a responsibility that I didn't live up to. I'm not going to blame God for my mistakes."

"Are you suggesting I'm to blame for what went wrong in *my* life?" Michael demanded.

"Of course not. But I don't know how you've survived without the Lord since then. That's what keeps me going. What will keep me going now."

He gestured at the ruins of the building. "In spite of this?"

"Perhaps *because* of this."

Her answer overwhelmed him. It was something he'd once believed, as well. The loss of his belief was suddenly an agony, as though he'd severed a limb. Even though it was being offered back to him, he couldn't accept, couldn't undertake that level of pain again.

"So what will you do now?" Michael managed to ask.

"I'll meet with the board."

"And?"

"And I'm not sure. We'll discuss the options..."

Michael knew there couldn't be many options, yet his strongest desire was to comfort Katherine, not add to her pain.

Somehow his arm was around her shoulders again. Together they watched as the rest of the neighborhood awoke. They listened to the sounds of surprise and dismay. And they both knew they needed a miracle...a multitude of miracles.

Meeting the next day, the board didn't exhibit the same degree of optimism Katherine did. The mood was dark, their confidence as destroyed as the church building.

Tom met Katherine's gaze, his own filled with both sympathy and despair. "I don't think we have many choices."

"We could try for a loan," she suggested.

"The bank has already demonstrated their unwillingness to extend credit," Roger Dalton replied.

"And we don't have enough money to consider repair or rebuilding," Don Westien added. "Even the carnival proceeds went up with the building."

Katherine grimaced, remembering again Michael's warning.

"We should have gotten fire insurance years ago," Tom fretted guiltily. "Right now, the large premiums don't seem so bad."

"We couldn't have afforded the premiums," Don pointed out. "So there's no point in wondering 'what if.'"

"I'm sure our congregation will rally to the cause." Katherine tried to buoy the group.

"If they don't, I'm afraid we'll have to disband," Tom replied solemnly.

"Oh, no!" Katherine protested.

"Without a miracle, I don't think we'll have a choice," Tom asserted.

"Then, pray for one." She glanced around to include the other members of the board. "All of you."

Discussion withered and died as they realized the gravity of the situation. One by one they left, until Katherine was alone.

Funny, her house had once been simply an auxiliary part of the church property. Now it was the only usable building they had left. But the tiny cottage wasn't big enough to accommodate a church meeting that involved more than a dozen people. Sadly, it wasn't an option for holding church services.

The idea of losing the church was unbearable. This pulpit had been very special to her. Almost from the first instant, she had felt Rosewood was the place she was meant to be, the place she would likely stay forever. It didn't seem possible that that could be taken away.

The doorbell rang, and Katherine wondered who it might be. Members, feeling a sense of disconnection and loss, had been dropping by nonstop since the fire.

But to her surprise it wasn't a member.

Michael filled her doorway. In his hands he held fresh daisies. "I thought you might be feeling down."

Nodding, she opened the door farther. "Come in." Accepting the flowers, she clutched them close, touched by his gesture.

After she sat on the smallish sofa, he took the place beside her. "How'd the board meeting go?"

She quickly filled him in on the details, trying to make them sound painless but not succeeding terribly well.

"I'm sorry. I know how much the church means to you."

"Oh, I'm not giving up. I know the Lord will provide."

"How can you say that? It will take a miracle."

"The Lord is capable of more miracles than we can imagine." She glanced out the window, and together they stared out at the charred remains of the church. "Far more."

Something deep inside cracked, a slow thawing fissure that Michael tried to hold back. But the feelings refused to be stilled. Feelings that told him he had to do something to help...for more reasons than he dared examine.

Of equal importance, Michael knew he couldn't allow Katherine this ultimate sacrifice. "I could help you rebuild," he blurted. "The bank would probably be willing to lend the money for materials, using the land for collateral."

Her eyes widened and filled with gratitude. "But it will take far more than materials, won't it?"

"I can talk to my employees, see if any of the men will volunteer a portion of their time or offer to reduce their wages."

"Do you really think they might?" Jumping up, she didn't wait for his reply. "We can call on the congregation for donations!"

He rose as well. "And for volunteers. Didn't you tell me you have a plumber on the church roster?"

"I did!" she exclaimed.

"Surely you have more skilled or even unskilled who will volunteer."

Katherine's eyes blurred, knowing that the Lord had provided the miracle she had prayed for. And not only in rebuilding the church. This was the first step in Michael's recovery of faith. He wouldn't offer to help if he didn't believe the church *should* be rebuilt. If he didn't feel the pull of the path he'd strayed from—if he didn't want to believe again.

Given a challenge, Michael was formidable. Several men in his crew volunteered their time. A few others offered to work and then wait to get paid until the church had the funds. As Michael had predicted, volunteers literally sprang from the church roster. Among them, Michael and Katherine were surprised but pleased to find, were several skilled workers. The work wasn't going as quickly as it would with a full-time, paid crew, but it was coming along.

And the bank, pressured by public opinion, had granted the loan for the materials.

Katherine restrained herself from reminding Michael that the Lord had indeed provided. She wanted him to see that for himself, to believe himself.

When she thought about the possibility of Michael regaining his faith, she was elated. But then Katherine would remember they were one miracle short. She still didn't have what it took to be a wife and mother.

And now, since that last concern had occupied her thoughts for weeks, she found herself crawling through the attic to drag down a trunk filled with old letters, diaries and pictures.

Back downstairs with the mounds of paper and pictures surrounding her, Katherine prepared to take one of her infrequent trips to the past. But the doorbell interrupted her reverie.

Opening the door, she blinked in surprise. Michael, Annie and David stood on her porch. She recovered quickly and ushered them inside. ''What a nice surprise!'' Then she glanced at Michael in sudden apprehension; Mrs. Goode was back to watching the kids when they returned from school. Katherine only watched them on the evenings Michael worked late. ''I thought Mrs. Goode was going to stay late tonight.''

''She did. We thought maybe you could use some company.''

David wandered near the sofa. ''Can we look at your pictures?''

Katherine glanced at the boy helplessly. It would seem cruel not to share her pictures with the children. But she knew from past experience that it could be difficult viewing the photos alone. With company, it might be downright unbearable.

Annie joined her brother, pointing at one of the pictures. ''Is that you when you were little?''

Recovering, Katherine nodded. ''Yes, it is.''

Michael studied her face, seeming to sense her reluctance. ''The kids don't have to look at your photos.''

Her past wasn't something she could hide any longer. It was part of her, part of who she was, something she couldn't deny. ''They can look. I'm afraid the pictures aren't very interesting, though.''

Crossing to the sofa, she handed David and Annie each a shoe box containing photographs. ''Can you guys carry these to the table, while I clear the couch?''

''Sure!''

As they scampered to follow orders, Michael stepped close, lowering his voice. ''I'm sorry. I should have called to see if you had plans.''

"I wouldn't consider sifting through the past as 'plans' exactly." Although it was strained, she managed a smile.

"Still—"

"No. I'm *very* glad to see you. It'll make going through the pictures more tolerable."

He looked puzzled, but glanced at the kids and didn't question her words.

Soon they were all around her circular oak table. Annie and David were fascinated by the most mundane photo.

"What are you doing here—?" David asked, holding up a picture.

She glanced at it, remembering. "My dad and I were fishing."

Annie peered at the picture. "Your daddy's looking at you like our daddy looks at us, when we're making him happy."

"Which is all the time," Michael told his youngest.

Katherine picked up the picture, studying it in a way she never had before. Could she have been making her father happy? The thought had never occurred to her before. All her family memories seemed a quagmire. Katherine hadn't believed it possible to make anyone in her family happy. Had she been wrong?

Glancing up, she saw Michael's gaze on her. Embarrassed, she put the picture down.

For the next few hours they sifted through the photos, evoking in Katherine more than memories. Strangely, she found she didn't mind sharing the experience with Michael and the children. Somehow it was comforting. And that was something she never expected.

"Do you feel like taking a walk?" Michael asked after they'd looked at many of the pictures. "It's a perfect night."

"The stars are waked up now," Annie informed her.

"Oh?"

"Uh-huh. Daddy says the stars sleep during the day so that they can shine so bright at night."

Katherine found herself smiling, appreciating this warm and thoughtful man who made everything so special for his children. "Then, we'd better go see them."

"Can we look at the rest of your pictures some other time?" David asked.

"I can't imagine anyone I'd rather share them with," she replied truthfully.

"I think I hear the moon calling us," Michael told them.

"Can the moon *talk?*" Annie asked, suddenly intrigued.

"Only if you listen *very* carefully," Michael replied.

"To the man in the moon," David added with authority.

Smiling again, Katherine grabbed a light cotton sweater from the hall tree. "I'm ready when you are."

"Let's go, then."

The kids ran across the porch and down the steps, the sound of their footfalls echoing over the ancient wood.

"Don't get too far ahead," Michael called out. Then he lowered his voice. "I think we've disturbed your evening."

''On the contrary, you've saved my evening.''

He reached for her hand, folding it in his own. ''If I'm treading where I don't belong, tell me. But I have the feeling you're troubled about something.''

She shrugged. ''Not all family memories are happy ones.''

''Are you referring to your own family?''

Katherine hesitated, her face pensive in the silver shadows of the moon. ''I'm afraid so. Just because my mother was a minister doesn't mean we were a model family.''

''I imagine it's more difficult with a minister mom than most others.''

Surprised, she stared at him. ''How did you know?''

''I didn't. But it's a fair assumption. That sort of career takes a lot of time and attention.''

''Which didn't leave much for her family,'' Katherine admitted in a choked voice. ''I admired what she did for the community, for the members of the congregation, but there was never any time for my father or me.''

''Yet you turned out pretty well. You even followed in her footsteps.''

Katherine shrugged. ''Yes. But unlike my mother, I know my limitations.''

''You? I find it hard to believe you have any.''

Katherine couldn't make her smile more than perfunctory. ''The same ones my mother had. Only, she was determined to have a husband and family even though she knew she couldn't give them what they needed.''

''What happened?''

"Eventually my father could no longer be merely a shadow, a prop for my mother's career."

"Divorced?"

Closing her eyes, she could remember the pain as clearly as if it had happened yesterday. "Yes. Their marriage was irreparably damaged from lack of care on my mother's part. I think my father stayed around as long as he did because of me. They don't speak anymore. And it's not out of anger, but lack of anything to say. There's no desire to exchange civilities at the holidays, no wish to resurrect a relationship that never should have happened."

"You sound bitter," he reflected in a neutral tone.

"I think a part of me always longed for a different resolution, certainly a different sort of childhood."

"Do you blame them?"

She considered this. "I suppose not. They were who they were. And it was in no way my father's fault. He married my mother, expecting a traditional wife. And she could never have been that. It simply wasn't in her. I guess the kindest way to put it is that theirs was a terrible mismatch."

"And so it makes you sad to look at your family photos, to remember how things were?"

She met his glance, a wealth of pain in her eyes. "Even more so knowing that's how they'll always be."

Puzzled, he angled his head. "With your parents?"

"No...with me. I'm the product of my upbringing, of the example I learned...and the profession I chose."

"You think your mother's failing in her marriage was strictly because she was a minister?"

Katherine thought for a moment. "I suppose it was

her personality—she was strong, independent and opinionated.''

''Is that bad?'' he asked mildly.

''I suppose not…unless you want a successful marriage.''

''And you think you have to be meek and mild to be happily married?''

Katherine paused. ''I don't know. But I am certain my mother's formula was a disaster. Which means I would be a disaster.''

''Isn't that a pretty big assumption?''

''Remember, I lived it.''

''From a child's viewpoint. It's not the same.''

''It taught me my limitations. I wish my mother had been so lucky.''

''So you would have traded for different parents?''

Startled, she snapped her face upward. ''I didn't say that!''

''Essentially. You can't have it both ways.''

She considered this, then met his gaze, her own unbearably sad. ''You're right. And neither could my mother. Which means I can't, either.''

Michael pulled her closer, his arm a protective shelter. It was a comforting gesture. One that spoke more eloquently than any words he could offer. They continued walking, letting the quiet and dark soothe age-old wounds.

Having circled the block, now they were coming up to the site of the church. Even though it was late, some men were still working.

''The response has been wonderful,'' Katherine murmured.

''It's what you expected, isn't it?''

She nodded, still staring at the activity. ''All of the

members have offered to help—even if it's just sweeping up, helping the professionals. And we've gotten donations from the hardware store, the lumberyard, and even the paint store. Yesterday the owner of the antique stop over near the highway called and offered us some old church pews. He said he'd rather see them in our church than in some New York loft.''

''It's amazing what can be accomplished when people pull together.''

She turned, her face brushing his shoulder. ''Especially you. I know you're working a killing pace between your job and coming here in the evenings and on weekends.''

He shrugged. ''As general contractor of your project, I'm bound by law to keep an eye on things.''

Her eyes darkened with appreciation. ''You've saved us a fortune by taking on that responsibility.''

''On the downside, it may take forever to finish the project.''

She brightened. ''We've gotten permission from the owners of the old school outside of town to use their facilities for services. They've been trying to sell the building for years without success. The owners think it might help for prospective buyers to see it used as something other than a school. They aren't charging us any rent—just the cost of utilities. But it'll be wonderful to come back to the old building once it's repaired.''

As they watched, the moon broke free from surrounding, slow-moving clouds. It seemed to shine directly on the church, as though in approval of the restoration.

"Even damaged, the church retains its dignity," Michael observed.

She glanced at him, wondering if this was a step closer for him. "Is it getting easier?"

But Michael couldn't yet voice his shifting feelings. He sensed the welcoming arms of the church. But in other ways, he still felt himself a stranger, one who had been turned away once again from a safe haven. And he wasn't certain that would ever change.

Katherine's hand curled in his. Michael suspected she thought the darkness concealed the vulnerability on her face. However, the same moon that illuminated the church also exposed her feelings.

The admissions about her childhood stunned him. No wonder she continued to withdraw. But now that he knew the cause behind her withdrawal, he was even further from guessing a solution.

One thing was clear. It wasn't only his lack of faith that stood between them. Katherine's past loomed large and unmoving. What were the chances of two miracles?

Glancing down at her unguarded face, his own was somber. That was about two more miracles than they were due.

Chapter Fourteen

"Our clothes are best!" Annie whispered, slipping one hand into Katherine's, the small fingers curling trustingly.

Katherine smiled. Learning that the other mothers and daughters would be wearing matching outfits, Katherine had sewn identical sundresses for herself and Annie for the Sunshine Girls mother-daughter luncheon. When Annie had invited her, Katherine had hesitated, not wanting to step on Michael's feelings by assuming the mother's role at the event, but Annie had pleaded. And when Michael agreed that Katherine should go, Annie was thrilled. He had planned an all boys' day with David so his son wouldn't feel left out.

"Did your mother sew matching dresses for you and her?" Annie asked.

Katherine laughed ruefully, remembering. "She could barely sew on a button."

"Then, how'd you learn?"

"In Home Ec—that's a class I took in school."

Katherine also remembered the award she'd been so proud of, the one her mother had dismissed.

"Will you teach me?" Annie asked.

"If you'd like to learn."

"Uh-huh. I want to make us more matching stuff."

Touched, Katherine hugged her. Then she straightened Annie's locket. Struck by a sentimental impulse, she had purchased matching gold heart lockets for herself and Annie.

Knowing that her role in helping the Carlson family would eventually be completed when Michael no longer needed her, she wanted Annie to have something to remember her by. She'd also bought a watch for David, ostensibly because she hadn't wanted him to feel slighted, but actually as a keepsake, as well. In her own locket, she had placed pictures of David and Annie. She hoped they would think of her once she was no longer a part of their lives. Katherine didn't know if she had a day, a month. When Michael found someone else to watch the children on occasional evenings, she guessed that would be the end of their association. Katherine knew the children would be in her thoughts often. They had relentlessly crept into her heart.

The children had been thrilled over their presents, not because their father wasn't generous, but because they were remarkably unspoiled. Michael believed in fairness, discipline and lots of love. In Katherine's opinion the formula was a smashing success. Even now Annie was reaching to stroke the locket, thrilled by the pretty trinket.

The luncheon went well. Everyone was presented with a single rose, and Annie kept hers close. They sang the Sunshine Girls song, and then the fashion show began. Teenagers and adults modeled the latest clothes from the local department store to the *ooh*s and *ah*s of the appreciative audience.

Annie leaned close to Katherine, whispering, "You're prettier than all the other ladies."

Touched, Katherine hugged her lightly. "Thanks, sweetie. I needed that." And she couldn't help wishing Michael shared his daughter's opinion.

After the fashion show, they strolled around the craft booths that had been set up around the park. A portion of the proceeds went to fund the Sunshine Girls. When Annie fell in love with a small wooden doll cradle, Katherine bought it. "We'll have to find something for David, too."

Annie nodded. "Okay. Maybe they have some soldiers."

There weren't any soldiers, but together they found the perfect thing: a framed picture of David's sports idol, Michael Jordan.

By the end of the afternoon, Annie was sated and happy. After they loaded their purchases into Katherine's car, the child reached up to hug her.

"Thanks for being my mommy today."

Katherine's heart flooded with love and her eyes filled with unexpected tears as she returned the hug. "I loved every minute, Annie." And every minute would be preserved forever as a treasured memory.

When they returned home, Michael and David were in the backyard, the barbecue blazing. To her surprise, the table was laid for four.

"Your world-famous hamburgers?" she asked Michael.

He grinned. "Proper macho food for our male-only day."

"But you have to stay and eat with us," David insisted.

She tried to demur.

"No excuses," Michael replied. "You wouldn't want to disappoint Annie and David, would you?"

Only the children? Not him? "Of course not."

"So what did you do on your all-guys day?" Katherine asked.

"We worked at the church," David told her proudly. "I helped doing sweeping and stuff."

Touched, Katherine gave him a hug. "I thought you were going to do fun things."

"It's what we wanted to do," Michael replied quietly.

Katherine met his gaze, just as Annie tugged at his sleeve.

"Daddy, look what Katherine bought me!" Annie told her father, showing him the cradle.

As he admired her new toy, Katherine handed David the picture she'd bought for him.

"This is way cool," David exclaimed. "Jordan's my favorite."

"Annie told me." Katherine smiled, pleased by his reaction.

Then Annie held up her rose, touching it to Katherine's. "And we got flowers, too."

"I see," Michael replied.

"I'm going to put mine in water," Annie declared, pivoting to run into the house.

"You don't have to buy them gifts," Michael said, as the kids scattered.

Katherine kept her tone even. "I know. I did it because I wanted to."

She waited for him to challenge the statement, but he didn't, instead studying her face.

Katherine wanted to turn away, to have him stop probing her expression, but she couldn't move. She was drawn into his gaze, the darkness of his eyes.

He stepped a bit closer.

Katherine swallowed.

Michael reached out to touch her rose, his hand barely grazing hers.

Feeling as fragile as the delicate petals of the flower, Katherine caught her breath.

"I was right. Beautiful women and perfect roses *are* found together."

Katherine felt something deep inside melt. Struggling against the feelings, she wished suddenly that the problems between them didn't exist. That they were simply a man and a woman. A man of faith who was ready for love and a woman who could accept that love without the constraints that now bound her.

But as much as that temporal wish filled her, Katherine knew it was not a solution…not even a consideration. Painfully, she stepped back.

Disappointment flashed across his face. Then he withdrew his hand. Immediately she felt a deep sense of loss. One she guessed would be with her for a long time. An incredibly and painfully long time.

A few days later Katherine's feelings were much the same. Despite her distraction, she brought her telescope to the Carlson home that evening since Michael was working late again. Mrs. Goode had been eager to leave. Annie and David were immediately entranced. Katherine had owned it since she was a child; remembering how much she'd enjoyed using it to study the night sky, she had decided to share it with the children.

"You can see stuff real far away!" David exclaimed.

"It looks like we can touch the moon," Annie murmured.

"I used to think I could," Katherine confessed. "And then my father told me about shooting stars."

"Shooting stars?" They spoke simultaneously in voices full of wonder.

Katherine smiled. "They leave a path in the sky that looks like a roadway to heaven." She paused, remembering. "My father would drive me around at night, and we would search the sky for them."

"Did you find any?" David asked.

"Sometimes." She smiled, thinking it was one of the better memories of her childhood, one she had preserved, one of only a scant handful.

"Could we do that?" Annie asked.

"Please?" David enjoined.

"Oh, I don't know. It has to be completely dark…"

"It's dark now," David protested.

"I know, but your father isn't home from work yet and I'm not sure—"

"Actually, I am home." Michael flicked on the lantern, illuminating the area. "I just got here."

"I didn't see you, Daddy!" Annie cried.

"Me, either," David echoed.

"I came in from the house through the patio, but you guys were focused on the telescope."

"You can see the moon and stars real close up," David told him.

"Hmm."

"And maybe we can touch them," Annie added.

He smiled. "Looks that way, doesn't it, princess."

"Katherine used to go looking for shooty stars," Annie replied.

Michael met Katherine's gaze over Annie's head. "I heard."

"And if you say it's okay, we could go look for some," David pleaded.

Katherine shrugged an apology, not wanting Michael to feel obligated. "It's late. Your father's had a long day at work—"

"But not too long," Michael interrupted. "We're going to look for shooting stars. Right, guys?"

Jumping up and down, they shouted with pleasure.

"So, how does this work?" Michael asked her. "We just point the car in the direction of the nearest star?"

But Katherine couldn't abandon her doubts. The more time she spent with Michael, the more difficult it would be to bid him goodbye. "You three go ahead."

"And who would navigate?"

Refusing to let her out of the excursion, Michael collected blankets and quilts, then put the seats down in the back of the SUV. When he was done, his gaze roved over her, his eyes full of questions he wasn't asking. "Is this how you did it?"

She swallowed the sudden nervousness that had erupted with just his look. "Well, it was a station wagon when I was a kid, but otherwise pretty much the same."

For a moment neither of them spoke, the silence stretching the night. Then the kids were surrounding them, small hands pulling at theirs.

Katherine tucked the blankets around David and Annie, and they snuggled into the makeshift beds. Unable to resist the gesture, she passed a hand over their heads, smoothing the hair from their foreheads. Their trusting sweetness caused a maternal pang so intense it was nearly unbearable. It also played havoc with her belief that she didn't possess any maternal urgings or abilities. Quickly she drew back, knowing she didn't dare grow any more attached to David and Annie.

Or their father, Katherine thought, once in the front seat beside Michael. The proximity seemed very intimate, very sheltered. Darkness enveloped them, as did the quiet of the evening. The children's voices were hushed as though noise might scare away the shooting stars.

Unable to still the motion, Katherine glanced at Michael. He turned his head just then, his gaze meeting hers. Was it the shadowy night that made it seem as though he, too, sought answers beyond their control?

He reached out just then, shifting into cruising gear. His hand brushed hers, and her breath caught. Swallowing, she couldn't tear her eyes away, as he reached over a bit farther, his hand taking hers. It wasn't an accidental touch, a bumping of fingers to be snatched back. Instead, her hand curled within his, the warmth reaching far beyond the simple touch.

Ever so slowly, she raised her gaze from their joined hands. His eyes acknowledged the connection. Beyond that, she glimpsed only mystery.

They continued driving, moving out of the neighborhood, past Main Street, until they reached the open fields at the outskirts of town. Without the lights from town to blend into the sky, the stars seemed clearer, even more enticing.

As the minutes passed, Annie and David remained entranced, whispering to each other.

Katherine was equally entranced.

With Michael.

It seemed they drove for miles, but no one suggested ending the evening. The stars, the sky, the darkness—all conspired to make the atmosphere nearly magical. They were moments too good to end, too fragile to disturb.

Katherine wished desperately that she could ignore her past...that she could hope for more tomorrows just like today, with the man now beside her.

The days passed. And although Michael was tired, it was a good tired. His current contracting job was going well, allowing him to spend more time working on the church repairs. He was pleased, but not especially surprised to find that the congregation continued to volunteer selflessly. Everyone from youngest to oldest had contributed in some way. Many of the elderly women had undertaken the task of preparing meals for the workers, freeing the younger women to act as construction helpers. And even the children swept and raked in the safe areas.

And something deep inside Michael continued thawing. He wasn't yet ready to put a name to what he was beginning to feel. Nor was he ready to name how he felt about Katherine.

Once again, she had been quiet all during dinner. And now, as the kids jumped on the trampoline, she continued to be uncharacteristically still.

"Problems?" Michael asked, wanting to get past the barriers she had erected.

For a moment her gaze locked with his, and again he thought he glimpsed that inexplicable expression, one he'd spotted a few days earlier—one that had haunted his dreams. However, she shook her head.

"Not really."

He didn't believe her, but just then Annie ran up to them, her hair flying behind her, her grin wide and open.

"Daddy! Katherine! Guess what?"

"What?"

"I jumped higher than David!"

Studying his daughter, Michael smiled indulgently. No doubt his son had let her win. David was a protective big brother, always looking out for his younger sister.

As though thoughts of David conjured him up, his son sprinted toward them, skidding to a halt. "Annie! You forgot this!"

Annie whipped around, reaching for the flowers her brother held. Then she extended the small bouquet. "For you, Katherine."

To Michael's surprise, he thought he detected a glimmer of tears in her eyes as Katherine accepted the flowers the kids had picked from the garden. She acted as though she'd received a precious gift. Then she hugged both children.

"Thank you. They're lovely. Just as you are."

Annie smiled, and David scooted his foot across the grass, embarrassed but pleased.

"How about ice cream?" Michael asked them, sensing Katherine needed an emotional break. He wasn't certain what had caused her to be so sensitive tonight. She claimed nothing was wrong, but he didn't believe her. She seemed more vulnerable than he'd ever seen her.

"Yea!" they both shouted.

"Yea?" he asked Katherine.

She clutched the flowers a bit closer and nodded.

It didn't take long for the kids to clamber into the SUV or for them to drive to town. And once they'd consumed their ice-cream cones, Michael suggested a walk.

The kids skipped ahead, but Michael purposely trailed behind.

"Is something wrong, Katherine?"

She shook her head. "My mind's just full."

"Worried about the money for the repairs?"

"Not really. Of course I'm concerned, but I have faith that the Lord will see us through this."

"Then, what is it?"

Her smile was at once sad yet mysterious. "It's funny how our past is so part of the present."

He angled his head toward her, wondering if he'd misread her expression, the reason for her quiet behavior. "Are you talking about me?"

For a moment surprise flitted across her expression. "No. If I wanted to talk about your spiritual needs, I'd be more direct."

"Your past, then?"

"It's not checkered," she responded, but her comment couldn't lighten the somber mood.

"I didn't think it was. But something's bothering you."

"Do you think you can overcome your past, the way you've been raised?"

Again suspicious, he closely studied her face. "Like in the church?"

She shook her head. "I mean relationship-wise. Or is our mold permanently set by the way we're raised?"

Not certain where she was going with this line of questioning, he was cautious with his reply. "My parents had a happy marriage. Hopefully I learned something from their example. I didn't really have a chance to find out."

She touched his arm. "I didn't mean to stir up sad memories."

"You didn't. Actually, it's getting easier to talk about. Ruth was part of my life..." Michael's next thought surprised him and the words came slowly. "Part of my past." He rubbed the bare spot on his ring finger where he'd removed his wedding band some weeks before.

Katherine looked surprised, as well. He could almost guess her thoughts. Was she, too, wondering if his broken faith was also part of his past?

Wordlessly, she extended her hand. Taking it, he wasn't sure if she was offering a lifeline or, impossibly, accepting one.

As the weeks passed, Michael tried to deal with his escalating feelings for Katherine. He could no longer deny that attraction had developed into something deeper...something enthralling...something terrifying.

Because to be with Katherine meant putting everything on the line. Not only his heart, but his faith, as well.

And while he searched for the miracle that could

allow them to think of a life together, he couldn't take the steps that would make it so.

At the same time Katherine continued to withdraw. It wasn't anything he could verbalize. In fact, she was even more tender with the children, always there for David and Annie as she continued to care for them some evenings.

But when she didn't know he was watching, Michael saw the pain in her eyes. When he'd tried to question her, she'd closed up completely. And his gut instinct told him more questions would simply drive her away.

Yet everything in him wanted to ask, to learn why she was distancing herself. So he'd tried to think of someplace where he could be alone with her, a place where she might relax and open up.

The roller-skating rink hadn't been his idea. And it was hardly an inspired choice. However, he'd promised Annie and David he would take them. He had thought of a quiet dinner with Katherine, even an intimate walk. Instead, they were surrounded by children, noise and a PA system that alternated between blaring announcements and teen idol music.

Annie and David skated like pros, zooming past them on their inline skates, leaving Michael alone with Katherine. Side by side, they maneuvered around the rink. Never a timid soul, Katherine took to the activity as though she skated every day.

Michael couldn't repress a grin. As usual, there was nothing restrained about Katherine. However, in spite of their skill they continued to bump into each other as they avoided younger, less adept skaters. But he couldn't complain, enjoying the proximity.

A bunny-hop gone wrong sent Katherine reeling. It

was only natural for him to reach out and steady her. He didn't drop her arm, though, instead snagging her hand with his own.

She met his gaze. Although the tension sparked between them in a nearly visible fashion, she didn't remove her hand. But he detected nerves when she bit her lower lip.

The younger set groaned when a strobe light came on and the music changed. The PA system spit out a golden oldie, and the song filled the rink—a romantic tune that seemed in keeping with the lovely woman at his side.

Their movements slowed in sync to the beat.

"How is it that music is like magic?" Michael contemplated aloud.

"I think it takes us to other times in our lives, hopefully to happy times," she replied softly. "They played this song at my prom."

"I bet you were the prettiest girl there."

She shook her head. "Hardly. I was at least a foot taller than all the boys in my class. And skinny. Not a teenage boy's ideal."

"They didn't know what they were missing."

"That's gallant of you to say so."

"Nothing gallant about it." He was amazed that she didn't realize it. But then, that was part of Katherine's appeal: lack of artifice.

She smiled, a curving of her lips that lit her entire face. "Too bad you weren't in my senior class."

"I don't know. I think you came into my life at just the right time."

A bit of alarm surfaced in her expression.

He reached for her hand again, to take advantage of the slow pace of the song that was playing. But the music changed again, a fast, loud tune that eliminated the possibility of conversation. Although Michael continued trying, he couldn't reach Katherine and he didn't know the cause of the sadness in her eyes. And even though he tried to tell himself it wasn't any of his concern, Michael wanted to know. He wanted to erase that hurt. And the reason he did so scared him to death.

Chapter Fifteen

"It's looking good," Tom said.

Michael turned away from his blueprints, then glanced at the structure that was slowly but carefully being erected. He couldn't stifle his pride at what he and the volunteers were accomplishing. "It's because of all your hardworking members."

"They have a stake in the outcome. We all do."

Michael wondered if the other man knew how Michael felt about Katherine, if the casual comment related to her.

But Tom continued easily. "Our biggest thanks goes to you. If you hadn't taken on the contractor's role, we couldn't even have gotten started."

Michael shrugged. "The church is important to Katherine."

Tom searched his expression but kept his own counsel. "That it is. I never imagined a woman preacher before meeting Katherine. Now I can't imagine Rosewood without her."

Again Michael nodded. He'd come to respect and

like Tom, knowing he was the kind of friend who could be depended upon. But he wasn't ready to share his feelings about Katherine or the church. "She's not going to rest until the church is completely rebuilt."

Tom chuckled. "Or you, from what I've seen. I hope you know how much we all appreciate this. We're all indebted to you."

"I'm here because I want to be."

It was Tom's turn to nod acceptingly. "I understand that."

Michael glanced at the kindly man but didn't see any double meaning. Then it struck him. Tom was simply acting like the church members he'd known all his life. He was offering fellowship, and Michael realized how much he'd missed that.

Relieved, he gestured over to the refreshment tables. "How 'bout some coffee and a sandwich?"

Tom ruefully patted his roundish stomach. "Never met a sandwich I didn't like."

Michael grinned, but before he could reply, Cindy sauntered over to them.

"Hey fellas. How's the Rosewood building team?"

"Almost as good as our softball team," Tom replied.

"So you're pitching again?" she asked Michael.

"Looks like it."

Her smile was wide and genuine. "Then we're sure to win this one, too. I'm going to grab some coffee, then I'm yours to command." Giving him a thumbs up, she strolled across the room.

Michael shook his head. "Yesterday she was climbing the scaffolding like a seasoned ten story man."

Tom smiled. "She gives the impression of glitz and

fluff, but that's not the real Cindy. She'll work harder than most laborers and not complain once that she's ruining her manicure.''

"Good. We've got plenty of manicure-breaking jobs.''

He glanced at his watch as they walked over to collect their sandwiches. ''It's later than I thought. I hate to keep everyone here so long.''

"You know you can't even chase them away. You've tried that before. They simply won't go.''

"True. You'd think they were being paid double overtime.''

Tom nodded. ''In a way they are. No greater reward than doing the Lord's work.''

Something inside Michael acknowledged the statement, but he was still struggling.

One of the women manning the refreshment table smiled at them as they approached. She was seventy if she was a day, but her smile was as perky as a youngster's. ''You boys must be hungry.''

It had been quite a while since Michael had been referred to as a ''boy.'' He couldn't repress a smile. ''Yes, ma'am, we are.''

Her gaze sharpened. ''You're the nice young man who's in charge of the rebuilding.''

"Guilty.''

Her smile was at once sweet and huge. ''Welcome to our family.''

Taken aback, Michael wasn't certain how to answer.

"It's a good one, our church family,'' Tom said, smoothing over the moment.

Again the woman smiled. ''We're thankful the Lord brought you to us.''

Swallowing a sudden lump in his throat, Michael managed to nod. "That's very kind of you."

"Nothing of the sort. Just the truth." Then she picked up a platter of sandwiches. "I'm Ruth. Ruth Stanton."

Michael's outstretched hand trembled a bit. And the lump in his throat grew. A woman named Ruth saying the Lord had sent him to this church?

"We have ham and cheese, turkey, tuna salad, roast beef, egg salad. And the soup today is vegetable beef."

Still rattled, Michael picked a turkey sandwich. "This looks good." After thanking her, Michael and Tom carried their food to a makeshift eating area. People had brought their own tables and chairs from home. It was an eclectic collection of everything from folding chairs to a few rockers.

Companionably they ate the tasty meal, but Michael couldn't shake the woman's words or the coincidence of her name.

Tom unwrapped his second sandwich. "Something wrong, Michael?"

Michael started to demur, then hesitated. Maybe he needed a sounding board. It was one of the things he sorely missed—the fellowship. "It's something she said just now."

"Ruth?"

Michael nodded, again struck by the depth her simple words had struck. "My late wife's name was Ruth."

"Oh," Tom replied in a quiet voice.

"That in itself isn't so remarkable, but then her words about the Lord guiding me to this church…"

Tom hesitated. "A crisis of faith?"

Shocked, Michael stared at him. "Did Katherine—"

"Absolutely not. You should know her well enough by now. She's loyal to a fault. It's just something I've sensed. Probably because I was in the same place not so long ago."

"You?"

"Don't sound so surprised. You're not a minority of one. My loss wasn't as significant as yours, but at the time I thought it was. The company my family had owned for generations was taken over by a corporate raider. Employees who had been with us their entire lives were let go, many losing their homes. Others had no other option but to leave town in order to find new jobs. I poured in every penny I had, to try to save the business, but it didn't work. And I was left with nothing. My wife was furious, and she filed for divorce. I thought the Lord had betrayed not only me, but everyone in our company who was counting on Him."

"But you've rebuilt the business?"

Tom snorted. "Nope. Not that I didn't try, but my credit was ruined, and I couldn't get enough capital to start a lemonade stand. So I took a job in sales."

"And your wife?"

Tom's laugh was brittle. "Long gone."

"Yet you're back, deeply involved in the church."

"God gives us free will for a reason. He didn't choose my wife. I did. And deep down I always knew she loved my money more than me."

"What about the corporate takeover?"

Tom shrugged. "I have to believe that His plan is greater than I can understand."

"And that's enough?"

Soberly Tom met his gaze. "I've never felt so alone as when I didn't have the Lord to count on. I may not understand the whys, but that's okay."

"Have you had doubts since then?" Michael asked, knowing his own crisis wasn't as easily solved.

"Not about my faith. It's hard to understand at times. Like now. A few years ago I'd have had enough money to donate a new wiring system to the church so the building wouldn't have caught fire. But apparently that's part of the plan, even if we can't understand it."

Michael blinked at the enormity of the possibilities. Without the fire, he wouldn't be standing in the church building, devoting so much of his time and feeling some of his doubts crumble. But surely... In an instant he pictured Katherine's face, and the longing that still lingered between them.

"There's a lot to understand," Michael finally managed to say.

Tom nodded. "Faith isn't static. It's only when we believe it is that we get in trouble."

"I never thought about it that way."

"I've had a while to think about it, to find my path again." Tom hesitated. "I haven't known you long, but if you need a friend who understands, you can call on me anytime."

Touched, Michael nodded. "I may just do that."

Only a few weeks had passed when Katherine glanced at the skeleton structure of the sanctuary, remembering when it had been aflame. Then it had seemed nearly impossible to believe it would rise again. She had always trusted they would find a way.

But she'd never guessed it would be in the form of Michael Carlson.

He had come to be part of the congregation even if he couldn't yet acknowledge it. He was known by name and greeted warmly by all the members. He was even pitching for the softball team. Offers to care for his children while he worked on the church had poured in by the dozen. And three members who had construction work planned for the future told him the jobs were his. One, a new restaurant, was a sizable job. Katherine had been gratified, but not surprised, by the generous treatment.

"Does it meet your approval?" Michael asked, surprising her.

"I didn't know you were here!"

"It's my home away from home," he replied.

Her eyes flew up to meet his, and the air vibrated with the tension his casual response evoked.

Regardless of the consequences, she reached up to stroke his jaw. Even though she was hopelessly in love with him, he still surprised her with his generosity and spirit.

"Katherine?" he said quietly.

Her hand lingered another moment before she drew it away. "I've been hearing a lot about you lately."

"I guess I could take that a couple of ways."

"Nope. It was all glowing."

He shrugged. "Just helping a good cause."

One that was pulling at him? "I agree."

For a moment the unspoken thrummed between them.

Then he glanced upward where the spire had once reached toward the sky. "So much in life is fragile."

Katherine's throat thickened; she knew he was right. "Which makes me appreciate it even more."

Again their gazes met, the emotion undisguised.

The breeze picked up slightly, ruffling Katherine's hair. She reached to smooth it, but Michael's hand was swifter. His touch, light but strong, lingered in her hair, its effect reached to her toes.

So much needed to be said, but neither could break the silence or disturb the precarious balance.

Michael's gaze flickered over Katherine again, and she sensed his frustration. But she couldn't continue their conversation. Their feelings were frighteningly close to the surface, and she didn't dare allow them to spiral out of control. Too much was at stake for Michael and his children. Too much for all of them.

For the first time in her adult life, Katherine felt helpless. And that she couldn't bear.

Chapter Sixteen

The following afternoon in the park was exquisite. Trees, decked in their October finery, practically strutted beneath their layers of changing leaves. And the sky was the blue lovers dream of. Even the pristine white clouds drifted by in lazy abandon. Mrs. Goode had needed the afternoon off—the kids had a half day at school. Fortunately, Katherine's schedule was clear.

She and the kids were resting on the swings. They had exhausted the slides, carousel and monkey bars. Usually about now Annie would plead for another round of all three. But she was unusually quiet. Though always a gentle child, Annie was typically filled with energy.

"Annie, is anything wrong?"

"I'm kinda tired," she responded, looking lackluster.

Katherine caught David's eye. "Then, let's head home."

Glad that she'd brought the car instead of biking,

she tucked Annie into the front seat. David didn't protest when he was assigned to the back.

By the time they arrived home, Annie's head sagged and she dragged wearily inside, collapsing on the couch. Katherine carried her the rest of the way upstairs to her room and then searched for a thermometer.

Usually healthy, the kids hadn't required any nursing while she had taken care of them. Katherine tried to remember now, what she could about her own childhood illnesses. Her mother's advice had been to buck up and get on with things. Her father had been more sympathetic, tucking her beneath a comforter, preparing soup, Jell-O and toast. And a humidifier had entered the equation a few times.

After helping Annie into her jammies, Katherine tucked the child into bed, covering her with a favorite, soft coverlet. Unable to find a thermometer, she placed her hand against Annie's forehead and cheeks. Flushed, they did seem warm. But Katherine wasn't experienced enough to know if the child was warm enough to warrant concern. After giving Annie some cool apple juice, Katherine phoned Michael.

He wasn't worried. "It's probably nothing to be concerned about. Kids get colds, and usually there's at least one in the fall or winter."

Not certain why, Katherine didn't feel completely reassured. "What if it's more than a cold?"

"If it's the flu, you do basically the same things," he responded.

"Should I call her pediatrician?"

"I really don't think it's necessary," Michael assured her.

"Do you know where the thermometer is?"

He groaned. "I broke it when I used it last on David. I meant to buy a new one, and I completely forgot about it. I'll stop on the way home and get one."

"She seems awfully warm," Katherine fretted.

"Don't worry. I'll cut it short and get home as soon as possible. Usually juice helps."

"I've done that."

"Good. Sounds like you have everything under control."

Katherine wasn't certain. After ending her conversation with Michael, she quickly dialed Cindy. Her friend's advice was to calm down, but she did suggest looking for the humidifier in the laundry room.

"Why?" Katherine asked.

"I'm not sure. Just that my mother kept hers there."

After ringing off, Katherine did find the humidifier in the laundry room. Not questioning her good fortune, she filled it and carried it into Annie's room. She wasn't certain it would help, but she doubted it would hurt. And doing something, anything, made her feel better.

"Would you like some toast?"

Annie shook her head weakly.

"A Popsicle?"

Again Annie declined.

Worried, Katherine pulled the wicker rocker from across the room, angling it beside the bed. "How about a story? Your favorite about the princess?"

"Okay."

As she read, Katherine stroked the child's hair, keeping her touch gentle. When the story ended, Annie latched her fingers onto Katherine's.

"You don't feel good, do you, sweetie?"

"No. Will you stay with me?"

"Of course. Do you want some more juice?"

Annie shook her head. "Just you."

Something deep inside melted, and Katherine knew that these children would forever be in her heart. Neither time nor distance could sever the feelings.

The minutes seemed to crawl by as she waited for Michael to come home. Katherine wasn't sure why, but some instinct kept clawing to be heard. She couldn't put a name to her feeling, but she was terribly worried. Perhaps she was overly concerned because she hadn't had children of her own, but the change in Annie seemed to warrant more attention than would a cold or the flu.

David was remarkably helpful, pouring more juice for Annie so that Katherine could stay by her side, then preparing his own sandwich.

"What would I do without you?" Katherine said, giving him a one-armed hug as she continued to hold Annie's hand. "You're so grown-up and responsible."

Pleased, he shrugged. "Do you want me to do something else?"

"Yes. Can you listen for your dad and let me know as soon as you hear his car?"

David nodded seriously. "Is Annie going to be okay?"

"Of course. It's probably a cold or the flu." Then it struck her. The last major illness in this house had been when David had lost his mother. She reached out again, snagging him in another hug. "She'll be just fine. You've had the flu before. It's really rough the first day or so. Then you get better."

"I guess so."

"No doubt about it," she reassured him. But inside, a yawning spasm of worry gripped her. Annie's breathing seemed a bit more shallow, her color a little worse. "David, could you bring me the phone?"

"Sure."

Annie appeared to be sleeping, and Katherine's nagging feeling had grown to mammoth proportions. She needed to know that Michael would soon be home.

As soon as David brought the phone and scampered back downstairs, she called Michael. But he didn't answer his cell phone, and she guessed he might have left the phone in his car when he'd gone in the store. She didn't leave a message on his voice mail, not wanting to add to his worry.

"Daddy's home!" David shouted from downstairs a few minutes later.

Worried, Katherine looked at Annie, but she hadn't even stirred at the noise.

Michael hurried up the stairs at David's insistence. His easy manner faded into concern when he saw his daughter's listless state. "Hey, princess."

But she was groggy, unresponsive. Quickly he used the thermometer he'd purchased. It read 104 degrees.

He met Katherine's concerned glance. "You were right. We should have called the doctor. Let's get her to the ER."

Within minutes, Michael carried Annie to the SUV, having already laid the seats down to make a bed. David insisted on coming along rather than being left with a neighbor, and Katherine backed him up. It would be more frightening for him to be left out of the picture than to accompany them to the hospital. Katherine used Michael's cell phone, however, to call

Cindy. Her friend agreed to meet them at the hospital and to divert David if necessary.

The ER doctor took Annie's condition seriously, immediately calling for a pediatric specialist.

"It's probably the flu, isn't it, Doctor?" Michael asked. "We wanted to be sure, but it can't be anything serious, can it?"

The doctor wasn't quick to reassure them. "Why don't we run some tests, Mr. Carlson. Then we'll know what we're dealing with."

Quickly the medical staff whisked Annie away, her body seeming incredibly tiny on the stretcher. And then Katherine and Michael were guided into the outer waiting room.

Cindy sat in one of the charmless vinyl chairs. Spotting them, she stood up, immediately making her connection with David.

Which was good because Michael looked as though he'd been sucker punched. Katherine took his arm, guiding him to a window.

"This can't be happening," he murmured.

"Michael, we don't know what's wrong yet. And you have to remain strong for David...and for Annie."

But he didn't reply at once, instead staring out the window. When he did speak, his voice was tormented. "This is how it started with Ruth. At first they said tests, just routine. Everyone reassured me things would be all right."

"This isn't Ruth," Katherine reminded him. "Annie's a young, healthy girl."

"It wasn't supposed to happen with her mother, either. She was strong, healthy. And then..."

Katherine touched his shoulder, meeting his gaze

straight on. "You have to believe that Annie will be all right."

"Have faith?" he asked in a tortured voice.

Although tears blurred her vision, Katherine nodded. "If not for yourself, then for Annie."

He bowed his head. "It's not a matter of pride, Katherine."

"It's a matter of faith, Michael. And you're the only one who can decide that."

Still agonized, he clenched his jaw. "I'll see what the doctors say."

However, over two hours later, the news wasn't good. Annie's fever was escalating, and she was having more difficulty breathing.

"Mr. Carlson, we're admitting Annie," the pediatric specialist, Dr. Thomas, told him.

"What is it?" Michael asked desperately. "What's wrong with her?"

"We don't know yet."

Michael gripped Katherine's hand. "You must have some idea."

"She's in respiratory distress, and we've ordered a comprehensive panel of tests." Dr. Thomas removed his glasses. "I won't tell you not to worry, because frankly her condition is serious. However, until we know what we're dealing with, I'd rather not speculate and have you worry needlessly. I will keep you informed every step of the way." He met Michael's gaze squarely. "And I'd like to take samples from your son, as well."

"You don't think—"

"Just as a precaution. We'll also check him over."

Michael nodded, but strain creased his face. Clearly he was reeling. Katherine felt his shock and pain, her heart absorbing an equal share. She could only imagine how alone he must feel without his faith to turn to. But she kept her hand firmly in his, emotionally shoring him up, incorporating him, as well as Annie, in her prayers.

For the next hour, they simply tried to deal with the shock. David finally returned and Michael hugged him fiercely. But then his attention splintered, obviously thinking about his youngest child. Cindy tried to engage David, but he had eyes only for his father.

"Michael, I think David needs you," Katherine whispered.

He nodded, releasing her hand. In moments he was at his son's side, looking collected and strong. "Davey, they're going to keep Annie here tonight."

Katherine watched, knowing how difficult the words were for him.

"Is she going to be okay?" David asked, his young face pulled into lines of worry.

Michael swallowed. No doubt he was remembering when he'd told David that his mother, too, would be all right. "We have to wait and see, son."

Katherine met her friend's eyes and saw the tacit agreement in Cindy's gaze. So she knelt down beside David and Michael. "If it's all right with your father, Miss Cindy can take you home for the night. Then you can come back and see Annie tomorrow."

"I have four kinds of ice cream in my freezer," Cindy told him. "And tons of video games. And you can sleep in a bed shaped like a sports car." She met Michael's surprised glance. "I'm lucky enough to have foster children on occasion. I keep the place stocked with kid-friendly stuff."

David looked between Cindy and his father, obviously torn.

Michael put his arms around David. "You'd be helping me, son, if I knew I didn't have to worry about you. And right now I can't think of anything I need more."

David took in the information with a thoughtful expression. Hesitating only a short while, he nodded before hugging his father fiercely. Still hanging on to Michael, David glanced up at Katherine. "But I don't think I should have fun while Annie's sick."

Katherine's heart caught at the love between these children, this family. She smoothed back the hair on his forehead. "Oh, I think Annie wants you to have fun. Actually, twice as much fun, for her and you."

David drew his brows together. "You sure?"

She nodded, the emotions clogging her throat.

Releasing his father, David clung to Katherine, hugging her equally hard.

Tactfully, Cindy stood, her gaze connecting with Michael's.

"Should we talk about school later?"

Michael nodded.

Holding Michael's and Katherine's hands, David glanced up at them. "You're *sure* I can come back and see Annie?"

Katherine glanced at Michael, silently pleading for him to agree. "Yes, David."

After the boy left with Cindy, Michael frowned. "I'm not sure it was a good idea to let him think he can come back to the hospital."

Katherine took his arm. "I know this is difficult to hear, but the last time someone in his family was put in the hospital, he was shunted off and told everything would be okay. And he lost his mother. Even if it's only for a short while, I think he needs to be here, to feel he's part of the solution.''

Michael's throat worked. ''What if there's no solution?''

Katherine felt her own heart breaking—for Michael's pain, for her own love of his children, for the agony they'd all shared. But hand in hand with the pain was her conviction, her certainty, that the Lord would help this family. Still, a solitary tear rolled down her cheek as she took his hand.

''We do the only thing we can, Michael. We pray.''

For a moment their gazes locked, the unspoken love thrumming between them, the promise of hope calling out to them, as well.

The nurse broke the moment, coming in to tell them that Annie was being transferred to the intensive care unit. She gave them directions to the unit's special waiting room. ''However,'' she concluded. ''Annie won't be back in the unit for some time. She's undergoing tests. If there's any change, we'll page you.''

''Intensive care?'' Michael whispered. ''That's the last stop before—''

''No!'' Katherine insisted. ''I won't listen to that. It just means she needs more care than they can give her in the ER.''

Michael covered his eyes with his hands, and she knew he was concealing his anguish.

She felt compelled to act. ''Michael,'' she pleaded gently, ''let's do something for Annie.''

Slowly he raised his head. ''What?''

Knowing where the chapel was, Katherine guided

Michael through the hallways. Once at the doorway of the small room, he balked, his torment clear.

A pair of tears slipped down Katherine's face as she held out her hand, knowing she couldn't decide this for him. Knowing she could only offer her support and guidance.

The pain in her chest multiplied as the moment lengthened. Just when she thought he was going to turn away, Michael took her hand. Closing her eyes, she silently thanked the Lord.

The chapel comprised a small altar and six equally abbreviated rows of pews. It was a place intended for prayer and meditation, and was usually attended only by visiting clergy and the family members of seriously ill patients.

Once seated, they bowed their heads. Katherine prayed not only for Annie's recovery, but for Michael's, as well. One physical, one spiritual—both equally important.

More than an hour later, Michael lifted his head and broke the silence. "I want to go and check on Annie now."

Sensing he needed to do this on his own, she nodded. "I'll either be here or in the waiting room."

She remained in the chapel, wanting to make sure he had enough time alone.

Then, needing to check on Annie herself, she returned to the waiting room. Michael stood alone by the window.

Hesitantly she approached. "Michael?"

He turned, meeting her eyes. "They've downgraded her condition. The doctor says it's touch and go."

Katherine's throat closed. They *couldn't* lose Annie. They just couldn't. "Did the doctor suggest anything?"

Michael's voice was even. "To wait."

"We can do that, Michael."

He met her gaze, his own revealing. "I don't think I could do this alone."

"You're never really alone," she reminded him gently.

He gripped her hand. "So you keep telling me."

As the hours passed, they waited for news. News that wasn't forthcoming. Alternately, Michael sat beside her, paced the small waiting room, and walked the corridors of the hospital. Katherine wondered if he'd sought out the chapel, but she didn't ask, sensing he was very close to the edge.

By dawn, they both were.

So when the doctor approached, Michael and Katherine stood with a mixture of relief and trepidation.

The doctor's face was somber. "I'm afraid I don't have good news. Her condition continues to slip. We're working to avoid lung failure, convulsions or a coma."

"Do you know yet what she has?" Michael demanded in a hoarse voice.

Katherine wanted to echo the request. It was incredibly difficult fighting this nameless, phantom illness.

The doctor shook his head. "Unfortunately, all I can say for certain is that it's a viral infection. We're treating it with antibiotics."

"Will that cure her?" Michael asked desperately.

"We can't be certain. To be perfectly honest, all we can do at this point is treat the symptoms, not the cause."

Again Michael looked tortured. "But how could she get so sick so fast?"

"It happens this way," Dr. Thomas replied. "I've seen a few other cases in the last two weeks. Comes on suddenly without warning and can reach the critical stage in a matter of hours."

"I should have done something sooner," Katherine murmured, guilt and worry consuming her.

The doctor allowed a flicker of sympathy to enter his expression. "You couldn't possibly have known. To be frank, in many of these cases the parents treat it like the flu, put the child to bed, and by the following morning it's too late. So, there's absolutely no reason to feel guilty, Mrs. Carlson. At least you brought her in as soon as you did."

Katherine gulped in relief. Only then did she react to his form of address. She opened her mouth to correct him, but Michael spoke first.

"What are her chances?"

The doctor hesitated. "We're facing a life-and-death situation. I've notified the school. They're checking to see if she's come in contact with any other children who have shown similar symptoms."

Michael took that blow, yet managed another question. "And if she makes it, will there be any permanent damage?"

Again the doctor hesitated, but sensing Michael wanted the truth, he met his gaze steadily. "Convulsions can result in brain damage. And comas are unpredictable. At the moment, our pressing concern is to fight the possibility of lung failure." He paused, his gaze flicking between them. "You can't do anything for her right now. Get something to eat. We'll locate you in the event of change."

Although they thanked the doctor, neither Katherine nor Michael could face the idea of breakfast.

And by lunchtime, food still held no appeal. Cindy brought David for a brief visit, but he couldn't see his sister.

"She may be contagious," Katherine explained. "Do you know what that means?"

"I can catch it," David answered solemnly.

"Exactly. And your father and I couldn't bear it if you were sick, too."

"Cindy let me have pizza twice," he confessed. "Is that okay?"

Katherine reached out to hug him. "It's perfect."

Michael's hug was even longer, more intense. "Will you stay safe for me, Davey?"

"You haven't called me Davey since I was little," the sturdy seven-year-old told him. "Except for last night."

"I guess I forgot for a minute how grown-up you are," Michael replied. "That's such a help to me."

"That's what Katherine said, too."

Michael smiled, holding him close for a moment. "And she's right."

The waiting room seemed very empty once David left with Cindy. And the hours passed with excruciating slowness. However, Katherine and Michael couldn't ignore the approaching darkness that eventually cloaked the windows in the waiting room. It signaled the length of their wait, one that still showed no end. They couldn't be certain if the duration of Annie's stay indicated hope...or a lack of it.

Michael stood, then glanced at his watch. "It's been twenty-four hours since we brought her in."

To Katherine it seemed like years since the previous evening.

"Do you think that's a good sign?" he persisted.

She rose to join him. "I'm sure it is." It had to be.

Michael looked out the wide bank of windows, even though nothing was visible in the darkness. It was as though the world beyond the shrouded confines of the hospital had ceased to exist. Then he turned to face Katherine.

"I've had time to do a lot of thinking."

Wearily she smiled. That was all they'd been able to do throughout the long hours. That and pray.

Michael met her gaze. "I've made a decision."

Katherine waited, suddenly sensing the importance of his words. As suddenly, hope and trepidation crowded her heart.

"Whichever way this goes, I know I can't live any longer without faith..." Michael's voice deepened to a near raspy sound. "I need the Lord to lean upon..."

Katherine felt the tears escape and knew she hadn't cried so much since she was a child. Gratitude and love poured through her, too. It was the miracle she'd prayed for. "Michael!"

Somehow she was in his embrace, their arms providing a mutual shelter. It seemed so right, so lasting.

When they finally pulled apart, he gently pushed back the tousled hair at her forehead. "I don't think I could have made my decision without you."

"It was inside you all along. You just had to work it out."

"Mr. Carlson?" The nurse startled them both, filling them with dread. "The doctor suggests that you see Annie now."

Terrified, they hurried after her into the hushed critical care unit. Here, no flowers relieved the sterile atmosphere and no laughter eased the tense surroundings. It was undeniably serious, unrelentingly terrifying.

The doctor met them as they approached. "I believe your daughter may slip into a coma. And I subscribe to the school of thought that insists this progression can be halted by the voices of loved ones. So, talk to her. It doesn't matter what you say, just that she knows you're here."

Annie looked so incredibly small in the bed. More frightening were all the machines and tubes hooked into her.

For the first time, Katherine wondered if Michael would crumble. It was a sight no one should have to endure, one that would destroy the strongest of the strong.

Katherine wanted to rush forward, to envelop this precious child, to hold her and keep her safe, to protect her from anything that might ever hurt her. As the parent, Michael must feel that a thousand times over. But something deep inside denied that thought. She couldn't love or care more for Annie if the child were hers by blood.

Michael took his daughter's hand. "Hello, baby. Daddy's here." He bowed his head briefly. "And Jesus is watching over you," he told her, ending the words in a strangulated sob.

Katherine put her hand on his shoulder, then leaned close to Annie's bed. "Hey, sweetie. It's Katherine." For a moment her throat closed and she wondered if she could go on. But she called on strength she wasn't sure she possessed. "You have to hurry and get well. Your daddy and I need to see your sweet smile. And

David misses you. He's eating pizza and ice cream and wants you to catch up with him.'' Even though she willed them away, tears blurred her vision, and she gripped Michael's shoulder so hard her fingers made indents in his jacket.

''You're my princess, you know that, don't you, Annie?'' Michael told her softly. ''And we need you more than you can ever know.''

''You have to get better,'' Katherine said through her tears, her voice choking. ''I need to hear you sing 'The Cross-Eyed Bear' again.''

Michael gripped Katherine's hand as the doctor approached, reading the data on her machines. ''No change. But that's not bad. The readings were steadily declining until now. You can stay with her a few more minutes, then we'll let her rest. In a few hours, you can come in again.''

Somehow Katherine and Michael made their way back to the waiting room. Losing track of time, they no longer knew how many hours passed.

A phone call from Cindy assured them David was fine. She also let them know that Annie's name had been placed on the prayer roll and that the entire congregation was praying for her. It was what they needed—a chorus of voices to heaven.

Tessa and her mother brought flowers that couldn't be taken into the intensive care unit. The child's large eyes were filled with worry for her best friend. Young Tessa had also brought her own favorite teddy bear for Annie. Promising to take the bear in to Annie when it was allowed, Michael clutched the stuffed toy, trying not to despair.

An anxious Mrs. Goode came by, as well, offering to watch David, to do anything she could. But there was nothing anyone physically could do. However, they gratefully accepted her offer of prayer, knowing it was added to the many other voices praying for their precious child.

The doctors changed Annie's antibiotics again in hopes they could fight whatever was gripping her. Michael and Katherine spoke to Annie two more times, yet there was no change. As evening approached, their worry intensified, obliterating everything else.

It was a situation that would try the most devout believer. And Katherine wondered if Michael would denounce his newly recovered faith. To her relief, although anguished, he suggested another visit to the chapel, drawing strength from prayer.

After counting the minutes until their next visit with Annie, Michael and Katherine practically bolted into the intensive care unit when the time arrived.

Annie was still lying quietly. Again they talked for some time. Michael held Annie's hand in his, willing her to live, begging the Lord to help her.

Katherine watched them, her heart lodged in her throat. As she did, Michael suddenly lifted his head, his eyes disbelieving. Katherine followed his gaze, her breath catching.

Annie's fingers curled slightly in Michael's hand.

"Baby?" he whispered in a plea of mixed disbelief and hope.

Although she didn't speak, Annie's fingers continued to gently move.

"That's right," Michael encouraged, his voice nearly cracking. "You have to stay with us."

Katherine couldn't believe it possible to feel the threat of tears yet again, but they filled her eyes, choking her.

The doctor approached. Katherine could only manage to point, unable to speak. Dr. Thomas spotted the movement Annie was making. Instantly, he checked the readings on Annie's machines. For the first time, light entered his expression.

"Does this mean she's getting better?" Michael asked.

Dr. Thomas glanced at them. "It's a cautious improvement," he said before leaving the room.

Katherine met Michael's gaze, hope flooding her own.

Michael's eyes deepened with another equally intense emotion. "I couldn't have handled this emergency without you either, Katherine. I couldn't have believed that Annie would make it. And I wouldn't have believed I could deal with it if she doesn't..." He paused, his throat working. "And I don't want to manage anything else without you in the future."

"Oh, Michael..."

His fingers were tender as they bracketed her face. "This may not seem like an appropriate time..." Briefly he closed his eyes, his fear for his child written across his features. Then his gaze met hers again. "But I never believed I could feel this way. And then there was you, changing my life, filling it in ways I never dreamed possible. I love you, Katherine, and I want you in my life—" his voice broke for a moment "—and my children's lives...forever."

Wordlessly she stared at him. It was what she'd hoped for, what she'd wanted from the moment she had grown to know what a wonderful man he was.

But she couldn't compromise his family's happiness with her inadequacies. They deserved so much more than she could give.

The nurse didn't chase them out when their time ended, so Michael continued to hold his daughter's hand. Katherine stood beside him, gently stroking Annie's hair. More than two hours passed. They watched her so intently that it seemed impossible their sheer will alone didn't awaken her.

Annie's fingers had stilled some time ago. When they began to move again, Michael jerked forward. Katherine's own hand flew to her mouth.

As they watched, Annie's eyelids fluttered.

Breath held, hope beckoning, they stared at her.

"Daddy?" she whispered.

Katherine's lips trembled, her face crumpling. This time she didn't even try to halt the tears sliding down her cheeks. Blindly, she turned to try to find the doctor. But Michael snagged her arm, pulling her close.

Annie's eyes opened fully. "Katherine?"

Katherine wondered that her heart didn't explode with love, relief and gratitude. Unchecked, the tears salted her lips, traced her face. "Yes, sweetie?"

"Do you want me to sing?" Annie whispered.

Katherine's muffled sob echoed against Michael's shoulder.

"Do you want to sing, princess?" Michael asked her, his own eyes full.

Annie's sweet smile surfaced. "For you and Katherine."

In a few minutes, the doctor formalized her prognosis. "She's on the road to recovery. Just as we don't know what caused the viral infection, we'll probably never know what cured her." He scratched his head. "It's nothing short of a miracle."

Katherine met Michael's gaze. It seemed impossible to believe. They'd been granted two miracles. Could they possibly hope for a third?

Chapter Seventeen

By morning Annie was remarkably improved. The doctor, believing the danger had passed, had allowed David to visit his sister briefly. Michael behaved as though he had a new lease on life.

Only Katherine was still wrestling with a problem.

She kept replaying Michael's words in her mind. For a moment she wondered if they had just been an impulse. But Katherine knew better. He wasn't the sort of man to make a proposal on a whim.

Michael had left for a few minutes to fetch coffee and make a few calls. But Katherine didn't mind. Not when she could spend the time in Annie's room while the child slept. It was such a joy to know Annie was improving, that she would be whole and well soon.

The door opened. Expecting one of the hospital staff, Katherine was surprised to see her mentor, Pastor James McPherson.

"Katherine." He greeted her in a hushed voice.

"James! What are you doing here?"

"I came to offer solace on the fire at your church. The note I'd written didn't seem enough."

"Oh," she murmured, realizing she hadn't given the fire or the subsequent repairs a thought.

"I was able to reach Cindy, and she told me you were here."

Katherine stroked Annie's hair. "This little one was awfully sick—" Her voice stumbled. "In fact, we almost lost her." Brightening, Katherine looked at him. "But she's going to be fine."

"That's wonderful." James searched her expression. "But something else is wrong. What is it?"

Her smile was tremulous. "You've always known me too well." She hesitated, again looking at Annie. "I'm afraid I've grown too close to her, and her brother..." Katherine glanced up at him. "And her father."

James's gaze was kind and understanding. "Why don't you tell me about it."

And so she did, pouring out what had happened, her own feelings, and Michael's proposal. Then haltingly she explained her background as well and the disastrous result of her parents' failed marriage.

"So you see," Katherine concluded, wiping away her tears, "why Michael and I can't have a future."

But his answer wasn't what she expected. "I'm afraid I don't. You've just told me you love Michael and his children. Not having an ideal childhood doesn't preclude you from being a good mother."

"How can you say that?" she demanded, expecting him to be the one person to understand.

But James's voice was gentle. "Katherine, I wish you could see what I do. A woman who has stayed beside the man and children she loves, one who even now can't take her glance from that child for a moment. You have fussed over her since I arrived. I don't think even a blind man would view that as indifference or inability. Whatever maternal urges your mother lacked have been given to you twofold. You forget, I saw you with the children before. You're wonderful with them, and they're obviously crazy about you. Katherine, your love for Michael and his children all but consumes you.''

Could he be right? Hope that had been nearly extinguished fluttered to life. ''But what if you're wrong?''

James placed one hand on her shoulder. ''I don't think that's the question. Search your heart, Katherine. I'll come back and visit you in a few hours. In the meantime, I'll be praying for you. For all of you.''

Katherine nodded, her gaze still on Annie. She heard the door close, and James was gone.

But that left Katherine with only her thoughts. Thoughts that whirled relentlessly.

What if James was right? Could she be the kind of mother Annie and David deserved? She'd never considered the possibility. Her past kept remorselessly slamming back into her thoughts. She'd seen others who had tried to outrun their pasts, but it seldom worked. Instead, marriages crumbled and families split. True, she loved Michael and his children, but was that enough?

The door opened again, and Michael tiptoed inside. ''How is she?''

''About the same. She fell asleep shortly after you went for the coffee.''

Michael handed her one of the foam cups of steaming brew.

She accepted it gratefully, latching on to the warmth it provided.

"You really should eat something," he told her.

She met his gaze, her own ironic. "So should you."

"When Annie's out of here, I'm going to buy us all the best meal in town."

Katherine's gaze flickered over Annie again. "I almost couldn't believe it when the doctor said it wouldn't be long till she can go home." Her lips trembled. "We have so much to be grateful for."

Michael placed his cup on the bedside table, then reached for her hand. "That we do. Katherine, I can't believe it took me so long to see the truth. I meant what I said last night. I don't ever want to lose you. I love you and I want you to be my wife."

It was everything she'd dreamed of, but what if she was wrong for him? He couldn't survive another blow like the loss of his wife. Katherine knew it was too much of a gamble. Michael deserved so much more...so much more than she could give.

Helplessly she stared at him in silence.

"Katherine?"

"Oh, Michael...I want only the best for you and for your children. And that's not me."

His voice deepened. "You don't love me?"

She bent her head. "There's more to consider—"

"What's more important than our love for each other?"

Again she stared at him, her own heart breaking. "It's more complicated than that..." Tears welled in her eyes, one escaping to slip down her cheek.

He reached up to wipe it away, his fingers as tender

as his words. "What can possibly mean more than our feelings?"

Just then Annie stirred, her voice weak. "Daddy?"

Michael tore his gaze from Katherine and leaned over his daughter's bed. "I'm here, princess."

"I dreamed we were at the park."

"We'll go there as soon as you're better," he told her, before raising his head to meet Katherine's gaze, his own both probing and promising.

"Good," Annie murmured. "I want to go on the swings."

"Then, swings it'll be," he replied.

His pager beeped, and Michael glanced at it, scanning the digital readout. "Looks like we have a problem at the site."

"Go ahead and check on it, Michael. Annie and I will be fine."

He smoothed the hair from his daughter's forehead. "That okay with you, princess?"

"As long as Katherine stays with me," she replied, slipping her hand into Katherine's.

Michael gazed at them both, finally nodding. But before he left, he leaned forward, his soft whisper reaching only Katherine. "I'll go, but we're not done talking."

She watched him leave, the hole in her heart threatening to choke her.

"Katherine?"

"Yes, sweetie."

"Will you go to the park with us to swing?"

The innocent words tore at her. How many more promises could she make to these children, knowing they weren't to share a future? "Why don't we see how soon you get better?"

"Okay. Can you tell me the pixie story?"

So Katherine did, relating the tale of the tiny pixie who fell in love with a leprechaun. Their love seemed impossible, yet in the magic forest the impossible became possible.

Katherine couldn't help wishing for a touch of that magic.

As she spoke, Annie's eyelids drooped and soon she was asleep. Katherine's heart filled with gratitude that their prayers had been answered, that this precious child had been saved.

A few hours passed. Michael phoned to make sure everything was all right, and she assured him he could take care of his crisis without worrying. The doctor had been by, again confirming that Annie was dramatically improving. Still, Michael promised to be gone only a short while longer.

But James McPherson arrived first.

"How's she doing?"

"Great, actually. The doctor thinks she'll be able to go home soon."

"Then, your prayers have been answered."

She nodded even though her lips trembled with emotion.

James met her gaze. "Perhaps not all of them?"

Katherine bent her head. "I'm so confused."

"So you've been thinking about what we discussed?"

"Truthfully, that's all I've thought about. But I can't dismiss my concerns."

"Do you love Michael?" he asked quietly.

She bit her lip. "With all my heart."

"Do you want him to be happy?"

Katherine nodded.

"And his children?"

"They mean the world to me," she admitted.

"And you feel that you and Michael are equally yoked?"

She knew that was now true.

"Then, all that's holding you back is your own lack of faith."

"Mine?" she uttered in amazement.

"You have to trust the Lord to guide you," James replied. "Just as you've advised Michael and many others."

"But…" Her protests died. In that instant she knew James was right. The same counsel she'd given applied to herself, as well. She had to trust the Lord. He would not have given her this wonderful man and his children to love if that was not to be her path. Gratefully she looked at her mentor and friend.

"How could I have been so blind?"

James took her hand. "Not so blind that you didn't finally see. I expect an invitation to the wedding."

The door opened. Michael entered, pausing when he saw her hand in James's.

But her mentor didn't falter. "You must be Michael."

Nodding cautiously, Michael drew closer. "Yes."

James smiled at them both, placing Katherine's hand gently in Michael's. "Then, this must be yours."

James left as quietly as he'd entered.

Michael met her gaze. "Should I ask who that was?"

Her eyes were bright, but this time the tears were borne of joy. "A very wise man."

"Oh?"

"One who agrees with you."

Michael looked wary but he didn't speak.

She swallowed, her heart so full it nearly crowded out the words. "He said you were right...that I should marry you."

Michael's expression was sober. "And what do you say?"

"Yes," she replied, unable to believe so much happiness was to be hers. "Definitely, positively, unchangeably yes."

His hands moved to frame her face. "I'll make you happy," he promised.

"You already do." Her heart hitched. "I love you so much, Michael."

His fingers traced the contours of her face, finally cupping behind her neck. "And I you, Katherine Blake, with all my heart."

Gently his lips touched hers.

Insistent light pushed past the undraped window, enveloping them, creating a golden, sun-stained silhouette of their embrace.

In the halls, the usual bustle of the busy hospital continued. Outside, people laughed and played in the park while traffic continued to fill the streets. But for Katherine and Michael, the moment was suspended in time. A moment only for them. One that only their love could achieve, and only their faith could sustain.

And one only their hearts could believe.

Epilogue

"Are you sure his outfit looks all right?" Katherine fretted, leaning over the carriage, fussing with the baby's clothes. It was still hard for her to believe that she and Michael had been married nearly a year and a half.

Michael smiled indulgently. "It's perfect. You made it stitch by stitch yourself. You *know* it's perfect."

"He looks pretty," Annie told her, skipping beside the buggy, her cheeks flushed with healthy color. Not a trace of her illness remained. She was radiantly, blessedly well.

"Boys don't look *pretty*," David told her, his hand possessively resting on the side of the carriage.

"I don't know," Katherine demurred. "I think he's absolutely beautiful, just like you and Annie."

David toed the sidewalk with his Sunday shoes, hiding his embarrassed pleasure.

"If we don't stop mooning over him, church will be over by the time we get there," Michael told his family. Yet, he, too, reached to smooth the baby's blanket.

"They can't start without us," Annie protested with a sidelong glance at Katherine. "We have the minister with us."

"It's a perfect day to christen both a church and a baby," Katherine mused.

The new building had risen from the ashes of the old. It possessed all the modern conveniences, yet they'd salvaged the original stone, the remnants of its beginnings, a sign of its history. Now the church was truly the best of old and new.

As was her family, Katherine acknowledged. Together, they blended as one. Her heart had never been so full, nor her gratitude so overflowing.

Katherine remembered the beautiful autumn day of their wedding. Michael had been impatient, insisting they not prolong the date. Although she'd had only four weeks to plan the wedding, Katherine was certain she'd never seen one more beautiful. Her dress had been a magical creation, and her long hair had been laced with fresh flowers and ribbons.

James McPherson had officiated. Cindy, as maid of honor, had beamed at her, eyes bright with joyous tears. Tom was both pleased and proud to be the best man. David, as their ring bearer, and Annie, as flower girl, nearly stole the show.

But Katherine couldn't contain her radiance when her gaze connected with her groom's. Remembering, she guessed the love they shared had been evident to all the guests.

In a gesture of peace and to symbolize the beginning of her new life, she had invited her parents to the ceremony. Her father, incredibly touched, had

proudly given her away. But it was her mother's reaction that had shocked Katherine. Victoria had wept
while the vows were exchanged.

And during the reception, Edward and Victoria had
taken a stumbling start toward ending their silence.
Her parents would never reunite, Katherine knew, but
it signaled a better future for them all.

Annie tugged at her dress. ''Are we really going to
be late, Mommy?''

Katherine glanced down at her precious daughter,
knowing a day would never pass that she didn't give
thanks for her very life.

Almost as soon as she and Michael married, Annie
had asked to call her Mommy. David had soon followed suit. And some days Katherine could scarcely
remember a time when they hadn't been her children.

''I think we'll make it, sweetie.'' Katherine
straightened the bow in Annie's hair, her hand lingering a moment. Then she draped it over David's
shoulder. ''You've already met Pastor McPherson and
his wife. You remember their boys. One is your age
and the other is just a bit older.''

''Are they still coming to lunch?'' Annie asked.

''Absolutely,'' Michael answered. He had become
friends with Katherine's mentor, and would always
be deeply grateful for James's words—the ones that
had convinced Katherine to venture into marriage.
And to finally have a family all her own.

Katherine paused as the church came into sight.
Her breath caught when she thought of the love that
Michael had poured into its rebuilding. He hadn't experienced a reluctant return to faith. Instead, he had
embraced it, weaving his belief back into the fabric
of his life. And he'd also pondered her earlier words

about the long hours he worked. Michael had hired a competent assistant, which freed him to spend more time with his family.

With Michael and the children hurrying her, they entered the sanctuary. A pew near the front had been reserved for them.

It was a new experience for most of the congregation—having a woman minister with a brand-new baby. *Ooh*s and *ah*s rippled through the rows of people. The entire congregation seemed to feel this was *their* baby, their family.

James McPherson and Jean greeted them with wide smiles, clearly pleased to be special visitors. At Katherine's request, James was performing the baby's christening. Together, James and Katherine would bless the new sanctuary.

Regardless of custom, Katherine insisted that Annie and David stand beside their brother during the christening. Both beamed with pride and love.

Young Danny, whose name was chosen because it was a combination of David and Annie, opened his eyes, seeking those he loved: his mother, his father and his very special siblings.

"We named him," David whispered to Pastor McPherson.

"After us," Annie added.

"Wise choice," James whispered back.

Then he blessed the youngest member of the Carlson family. Katherine tried to blink back the tears, but her joy was too great. Again she gave thanks for her incredible husband, their children, their abundance of gifts.

Meeting Michael's eyes, she found the reflection of her own feelings. He held their son, his large, strong hands incredibly gentle as they dwarfed the small head and body.

And somehow, Katherine fell in love with Michael all over again.

The music swelled, filling the sanctuary. Sunlight pierced the stained-glass windows, casting the most beautiful of shadows, prisms of shattered color that laced the pews.

Katherine's gaze locked with Michael's. Love bound them, a love so consuming that even now it made her breathless. To her wonder, his glance alone could reach out and touch her, conveying all the emotions she'd once despaired of knowing.

The tender look between them lingered.

Hearts filled beyond expectation, they celebrated this newest miracle, knowing they had received miracles without measure. And they'd only just begun.

* * * * *